RIDERS OF THE TROJAN HORSE

RIDERS OF THE
TROJAN HORSE

Lauran Paine

GUNSMOKE

This hardback edition 2009
by BBC Audiobooks Ltd
by arrangement with
Golden West Literary Agency

ISBN 978 1 405 68281 7

All the characters and events portrayed in this work
are fictitious.

British Library Cataloguing in Publication Data available.

Printed and bound in Great Britain by
CPI Antony Rowe, Chippenham and Eastbourne

CONTENTS

1

An Angry Man

WHITNEY Pierson held a shotgun in both hands as he stood on the off-side of the stagecoach he'd tooled into Beaverton. He was a dark-eyed, stocky man in his late forties, of average height with a close-cropped dark beard, a weathered countenance, and right now he not only looked embarrassed, he felt embarrassed. He was a stage driver, not a gunguard. People on the far plankwalk looked over at him, some grinned, and one man, a large, thick individual with a gold watch chain across his middle, called out, "Hey, Whit. You're scarin' folks to death."

The laughter was loud enough to bring merchants to their roadside doorways to stare, to join the little crowd that had gathered, and to react with more amusement. One of them, a local saddle and harness maker named Tom Hart, a card-playing whiskey-drinking friend of Whit Pierson, stepped to the very edge of the walkway.

"You ought to be ashamed," Hart said, "frightenin' folks like that. That thing ain't loaded is it?"

Whit glared. On the opposite side of his coach three men from the Beaverton Banking Company were unloading six small, very heavy oaken boxes that had been reinforced with steel. Until they finished, Whit had to stand guard.

Marshal Given, a lean, graying man with a beaked nose and flinty gray eyes, came walking northward from the jailhouse. He stopped, tipped down his hat to provide shade, and after a moment of watching, struck out on a diagonal

1

course in Pierson's direction. When he got over there the marshal stopped, hooked thumbs in his shellbelt, regarded Pierson stonily, and said, "What do you think you're doing?"

Whit jerked his head. "Go around on the other side and ask Mister Bonner. It was his idea."

The marshal walked away. Whit grounded the shotgun, leaned it aside, and felt for his tobacco plug. Most of the spectators across the road drifted away. Tom Hart rubbed both hands on his stained, wax-stiff harness-maker's apron, muttered something snide to the large man with the gold watch chain, and went back into his shop. The large man also departed, heading in the direction of the general store, which he owned. His name was Walter Coggins. He was, among other things, chairman of the town council, with one more year to go on his two-year stint.

The marshal came back around where Pierson was standing beside the shotgun, rhythmically chewing. They exchanged a look and the lean man almost smiled. "If the stage company wasn't so damned miserly they'd have had a gun-guard ride with you. Then you wouldn't have had to stand here for everyone to laugh at."

Pierson turned aside to expectorate and did not face the lean man again, although he spoke to him. "Marshal, in all my life I never yet bit the hand that fed me. If you got reason to raise hell with the company, right over yonder is the corralyard gates. Me, I got nothing to say."

The marshal ran a slow glance both ways along Main Street, settled against the coach at his back, and sighed. "You know why most robberies happen, Whit? Because someone like Charley Bonner figures that a shipment of new money to his damned bank will be safe as long as he don't take anyone into his confidence, including the local law." The marshal turned to gaze at Pierson. "If you ever do this again, for crissake don't stand out here in plain sight, get inside the coach. If anyone wanted to make a raid while that money was being offloaded, you'd be a sitting duck."

Pierson felt his neck getting red. He looked straight across the road in the direction of Tom Hart's leather-goods store. "If someone tries to talk me into doing this again," he stated flatly, "I'll hand them the shotgun an' go home to supper."

A perspiring older man, bald as a bird's egg, who had a pink complexion and washed-out pale blue eyes came around to where Marshal Given and Whit Pierson were leaning. Charley Bonner mopped his face with a large white handkerchief as he said, "It's all inside, Whit. I'm right obliged to you." He swung a pale glance in the lawman's direction. "I'd appreciate if you'd look in at the bank last thing tonight before you head for the rooming house."

Pierson passed the shotgun to the bald man and started up from the wheel hub to the driver's boot of his outfit. He did not speak or look down to see if they were clear of his coach as he sat down, unwound the lines, kicked off the binders, and whistled up his hitch. He had to go to the southerly end of town and beyond before he found enough room to turn the stage around and head back up through to reach the wide opening into the corralyard.

Two hostlers were waiting, grinning from ear to ear, both too prudent to say a word as Pierson climbed down, tossed his lines to one of them. As he stamped toward the company's office he pulled off his smoke-tanned leather gauntlets, the symbols of his seniority as a coach driver.

There was a coal-oil lamp burning, even though it was still mid-afternoon, and the man hunched at an old desk wearing a green eyeshade had to lean far back and remove thick eyeglasses before he knew who had entered his working area. He smiled through a straggly dragoon mustache, raised bent fingers to scratch a thin crop of nondescript hair, and said, "I saw you over there, standing guard while they unloaded. That wasn't my idea, so don't go lightin' into me."

"You knew that money would be on my coach. You damned well knew it wasn't trade beads in those boxes, Sam."

Sam leaned farther back, still grinning. "That was the

point, Whit. Like Charley said, if no one knew, not even you, then there wouldn't be no trouble. And, by gawd, he was right."

Pierson loosened his heavy coat, thumbed his hat back, and regarded the amused man behind the desk. "Sam, suppose someone up north had found out I'd be carryin' that shipment by myself, with no gun-guard?"

"But no one did, Whit. You came through slick as a greased pig."

Pierson looked at the floor for a moment before speaking again. "I don't know which of you sons of bitches is the stingiest, but I'm not goin' to the trouble of finding out." He walked as far as the roadside door and, while gripping the latch, said one more thing. "You got me scheduled for the five-o'clock run south in the morning?"

"Yes. Like always."

"Well now, you get someone else to take it south because I don't work for the Beaverton Stage and Cartage Company anymore."

He slammed the door so hard behind himself that Sam, who had tilted back in his chair, had to lunge forward to avoid going over backward when the building shook.

Evening was on the way; roadway and sidewalk traffic was down to a minimum. Pierson had to pause in crossing the road until Doctor Muller went past in his dusty top-buggy. Muller's big old stud-necked Morgan mare was stepping right along, eyes fixed on the livery barn where she was boarded.

As they passed, the heavy, older man leaned out and raised a hand as he said, "Whit."

Pierson nodded back. "Carl."

Across the road Tom Hart was entering Doughbelly Price's saloon, the Beaverton Waterhole. Price's name was Franklin, but most folks around the territory called him Doughbelly. He was of slightly less than average height and had a paunch that hung over his belt.

When Whitney Pierson entered, Doughbelly and Tom Hart were laughing over something Hart had just said. They stopped laughing, and Doughbelly reached for a clean jolt-glass to place beside the bottle in front of the harness maker. Whit gave them both a sulphurous look, nodded curtly, and filled his glass before opening his mouth.

"That trick this afternoon was so goddamned funny I quit," he said and, ignoring the startled looks he got, raised his glass, tipped his head back, and dropped the liquor straight down. As he pushed the glass aside and leaned over the bar, the harness maker recovered from his astonishment. "Quit? You mean you quit drivin' for Sam?"

"Yep."

There was a long moment of silence during which a stranger came in, bought a jolt of whiskey, nodded, and departed. Ordinarily his arrival and departure would have stirred some speculative interest. This time it didn't. Dough-belly fished glasses from a bucket of greasy water and began drying them. He and Tom Hart exchanged a look and a shrug. Doughbelly had nothing to say. He and Whit Pierson had been friends for years, but Doughbelly had been a saloonman a lot longer. He had learned very early never to ask questions of someone who might be upset.

Tom Hart was different. He was over six feet tall, did not weigh quite a hundred and seventy pounds, was grizzled, rough, and tactless. He and Whit Pierson had arrived in Beaverton the same time, close to twelve years earlier. They had been friends that long too, so Tom felt impelled to comment. He refilled his little glass but made no move to raise it.

"Hell, Whit. A man's got to take a little ky-yiing. We was just havin' some fun. You shouldn't quit over a few folks teasing you out there."

Pierson was watching Doughbelly polish glasses. "That's not it," he said shortly, and turned to eye his old friend. "Those two damned misers, Sam Holt at the stage company and Charley Bonner at the bank—they could have got me killed because they were too stingy to hire a guard to ride with me. An' they didn't even tell Jack Given a load of money was comin' for the bank. What's the good of havin' a lawman if you don't let him know when something like a money shipment is on the way?"

Doughbelly went right on polishing glasses, occasionally glancing in the direction of the roadway spindle doors. Suppertime was about over; soon more customers should be drifting in.

Tom Hart offered to refill Pierson's glass. The stage driver relented just enough to shove the glass over, but as it was being refilled, he said, "That Charley would do something like that didn't surprise me, but Sam—so help me Hannah, I been pullin' him out of bad situations with his damned coaches for more'n ten years—I never thought Sam'd take a chance on gettin' me killed just because Charley was too cheap to pay for a guard."

Several townsmen drifted in, one at a time except for Marshal Given, who had Walt Coggins from the general store with him. They were both tall men, but Coggins's overall fleshiness contrasted starkly with Jack Given's sinewy leanness.

Doughbelly went up the bar to serve them, but when the storekeeper said something and chuckled, Doughbelly shook his head and gave Coggins a warning look. In a half-whisper he said, "I'd leave it lie, Walt. He quit Sam, and right now I don't think you ought to badger him."

Both men stared at Doughbelly, then turned to gaze down where Whit and Tom Hart were quietly talking. Marshal Given faced back with raised eyebrows. "He's been nursemaiding Sam's rigs since before I come here. It's sort of like a tradition, Whit in them smoke-tanned big gloves of his, comin' into town sittin' straight up on one of Sam's rigs."

Coggins downed his drink and pushed the glass away. He never had more than one jolt when he stopped by after

locking up for the night and before heading home for
supper. He brought forth a cigar, bit off the end and spat it
aside, plugged the stogie into his mouth, and chewed. He
never lighted cigars. He had been a tobacco chewer for years
before marrying. After that, because his wife raised so much
Cain about his chewing, he gave up cut plug and took to
cigars. His wife said tobacco chewing was not only a filthy
habit, it wasn't genteel.

Coggins spoke quietly around his cigar. "He'll get over it.
He'll sulk for a day or two, then go back."

Marshal Given gazed at the little sticky pool he was turning
his glass in. He did not agree. "I don't know, Walt. I sort of
doubt it. You fellers have known him longer'n I have, but
when it comes to judgin' men I didn't come down in the last
rain. Whit's a stubborn individual. If he figures he's been
done wrong, he won't forget it."

Coggins pulled out a big gold watch, flipped the case open,
consulted the spidery black hands, repocketed the watch,
and said, "I got to get home. Well, what's he going to do?
He's a driver. He knows rigs and horses, harness and such
like. Sam's got the only business in town that uses drivers."

Doughbelly offered his thoughts about this. "He isn't married, don't have no family around here. He lives alone in that
little house he bought behind the blacksmith's shop. My
guess is that Whit's saved a little money. He can get along for
a while, even if he don't hunt another job."

Coggins slapped Marshal Given lightly on the shoulder as
he was turning away. "Got to go. See you gents tomorrow."

They watched him disappear beyond the roadway doors,
and Doughbelly wagged his head. "He done it to you again,
Jack."

Marshal Given nodded while sorting silver coins on his
palm to pay for the drinks. "He sure as hell did. I'll tell you
one thing, Doughbelly—Charley Bonner and Sam Holt
aren't the only stingy bastards around here."

2

The Day After

IN a place like Beaverton where everyone knew everyone else, it never took long for gossip to spread, even to the outlying cattle outfits, because every few days this time of year ranch wagons came into town for the mail and supplies.

Sam Holt went over to the bank, where Charley Bonner greeted him with a broad smile. "Went off like clockwork," he crowed, gesturing in the direction of a massive steel safe on rollers that stood in a corner. Empty money crates were stacked beside it. "You can pick up the boxes and send 'em back any time you're of a mind to."

Sam removed his thick glasses and polished them on a large blue bandanna as he said, "Whit quit me right after he brought the stage in yesterday afternoon." He finished with the glasses and adjusted the steel frames over his ears. He could see Bonner better now. The banker was staring at him, no longer smiling. Sam did not smile either. "That's something I didn't count on when I agreed to let him fetch the money without a guard."

Bonner spread fleshy hands. "It worked, didn' it?"

"Yeah. Only Whit was madder'n a hornet about you an' me usin' him like that. He said we could have got him killed."

The banker reddened. "Nothing happened, Sam. He should be pleased."

"Maybe. But he isn't. He figures we set him up. No one likes somethin' like that. Only I didn't think that far ahead. I just figured your scheme would work. I didn't figure Whit'd take it so personal."

Bonner gazed out the front window where roadway traffic was brisk. "Get another driver," he said, and brought his gaze back to the stage company's owner. "Who in hell does he think he is, anyway?"

Sam Holt's eyes looked large through the thick lenses of his glasses. "Where?" he asked shortly. "I use three drivers. Two are out on runs. Whit was scheduled to go south this morning."

Bonner was tiring of this discussion. "There are other teamsters around," he said.

Holt made a little death's-head grin. "Charley, you been sittin' inside this bank too long. Teamsters aren't stagecoach drivers. Teamsters drive wagons. I can think of about five, six teamsters in the territory. I wouldn't trust one of my outfits with any of them."

"Well, who took Whit's coach out this morning?"

"No one. It's sittin' over there in the yard. There was a lady and two gents to go south, paid up and ready. They wasn't very happy when I told 'em the stage wouldn't be leavin' town because the driver quit an' I don't have anyone to take his place."

The banker looked steadily at Sam Holt, his earlier pleasantness diminishing by the second. "Are you blamin' me because he quit?"

"It was your idea to sneak the money down here on an everyday run."

"Sam, damn it all, it's your stage company. You make the decisions."

Holt nodded. "That's right, and from now on if you want to charter a coach you're goin' to pay wages for a gunguard."

Charley Bonner watched Holt walk out into the roadway, blew out a big breath, and returned to his desk behind the wicket, where an expressionless clerk was transacting bank business. He sat down, unconsciously fidgeted with his massive gold watch chain for a moment, then grunted. Putting the affair of Whit Pierson out of his mind, he went back to work.

It was not that simple for Sam Holt. When he got back to the office Marshal Given was sitting cocked-back near the stove.

Givens nodded when Holt walked in, waited until he was seated behind his desk, then said, "That was an underhanded thing you did, Sam. Whit's a driver, not a gun-guard. If there'd been a raid yesterday with him standing on that stage with a scattergun, they would have shot him out from under his hat first thing."

Holt adjusted his glasses and glared across the room. "I don't need this from you too," he exclaimed, then paused, relaxed a little, and rested both arms atop the littered desk. He resumed in a normal tone. "I just came from the bank. I told Charley that any time he uses one of my rigs after this he's goin' to have to pay for a guard."

Marshal Given's expression did not change. "That's only part of it," he stated. "You'n Charley could have got a lot of folks killed yesterday. Every other time money came into town I was told it was on the way. Yesterday—"

"That was Charley's idea. He said if only him and me knew, it'd cut the risk of a raid by two thirds."

Given brought his chair down off the wall with a sharp sound and shot up to his feet. It was common knowledge around the countryside that when Jack Given was angry, the wisest policy was not to add to his aggravation. Sam Holt leaned back and looked up. "It won't happen again, Jack. An' if you see Whit, tell him for me I'll up the ante if he'll—"

"If you got something to say to him, do it yourself," snapped the lawman, then walked out into the sunshine, leaving Sam Holt feeling miserable as he regarded the closed roadway door.

The marshal was crossing the road in the direction of the

general store when Charley Bonner hailed him from the bank's doorway. Given changed course and stepped up onto the duckboards a few feet from the banker; neither nodded or spoke. Given hooked both thumbs in his shellbelt and stood waiting.

Bonner's color began climbing again. He did not require an admonition from the town marshal, so he said, "All right. But you got to admit it worked. Three thousand dollars in new money all the way from the Denver mint without even a whiff of trouble."

Given was choosing his words. After all, this would blow over, but Charley would still be head of the town council, the outfit that paid the marshal's wages.

He said, "It was a damned fool thing to do. Least of all you could have told *me* the money was coming. If there'd been a raid, I might have been out in the countryside somewhere."

Bonner hung fire for a moment. He was beginning to be less defensive about this entire affair. All the jawboning he'd had about it since yesterday did not change the simple fact that the money was safely in the bank's big steel box. But he did not want to argue with Jack Given, so he said, "Next time I'll pay for a guard. Now let's talk about something else. For instance, only a thousand dollars of that money stays here; the other two thousand goes to the bank down in Livermore."

Given's brows climbed. "Why wasn't it sent down there in the first place?"

"Because Whit come in late and I didn't like the idea of it goin' south on the night stage. But it's got to be delivered within the next few days. They'll be wondering where their money is."

Given regarded the large fleshy man stonily. "Who is going to take it? Whit quit an' Sam's other two drivers are—"

"I know all that," Bonner said, letting his head list slightly to one side in a speculative manner. "The reason I called you over was because I know how you can earn some extra money."

Jack Given's expression changed. "Me? You want me to deliver that money to Livermore?"

"It's not that much of a job. Sam's got to send out a southbound coach. He's got passengers waitin' to go. And you drove stages in Idaho. That's what you told the town council when they hired you sometime back. Jack, it's worth forty dollars. You can make your monthly wage in one day—well, one afternoon and one night, then you come back. A day and a half. At most, two days."

Marshal Given turned slightly to look in the direction of his jailhouse. He fixed his gaze on a pair of rangemen riding up through town from the lower end. He leaned to expectorate into roadway dust, then he faced Charley Bonner again. "Fifty dollars."

"That's highway robbery!"

"Fifty dollars, Charley, and you pay the wages of a gunguard."

Bonner's neck swelled, his eyes widened. "Livermore is only twenty-five miles south. You can make the delivery and be back home by tomorrow afternoon."

"And suppose trouble busts out here in town while I'm in Livermore?"

"Why should it? Tomorrow won't be Saturday. Anyway, if there's an emergency and you're not around, we got the town possemen."

"Does Sam know about this?"

"No. Nobody knows but me and the folks at the Livermore bank. And you."

"Someday," stated the lawman quietly, "you're goin' to outsmart yourself, Charley. Someday your darned secretiveness is goin' to land you up to your withers in trouble."

Bonner's reaction to being spoken to like this was unusual. He normally got loud and angry when someone crossed him. This time, although the vein in the side of his neck pulsed strongly, he forced a smile. "A man lives and learns. Next time I'll let you know, and I'll see that a guard rides the coach. But right now what we're talkin' about is a short run with passengers, just like an ordinary coach. Jack, it wouldn't have cost the bank no fifty dollars if I'd put a guard on the stage with Whit."

Given barely inclined his head. "Yeah. I know that. That's why I set the figure at fifty plus the gun-guard. To teach you a lesson."

Bonner regarded the tall lean man in silence for a moment or two, then spread his hands and smiled again. "All right. Fifty to you and a gun-guard. When can you leave? It's close to midday already."

"First, you better go let Sam know. I can tell you for a fact he's particular about who he lets tool his stages and handle his horses. He might not like the idea. I'll be at the saloon. If he agrees and will see that the coach is got ready, I can leave within the hour."

Marshal Given headed for the saloon. Charley Bonner watched him briefly before crossing toward the corralyard.

Inside the saloon, Doughbelly Price was reading a rumpled, old newspaper when the marshal entered. There were three old men playing toothpick poker near the front window, and Whit Pierson was nursing a five-cent glass of beer, listening to an article Doughbelly was struggling through that had to do with Indian trouble down in New Mexico Territory.

Doughbelly carefully folded the paper, got down off his back-bar stool, and nodded at the marshal. "Beer?"

Given settled at the bar, nodded to Whit Pierson, who nodded back. Then the marshal put a five-cent coin atop the bar and said, "Beer." As Doughbelly walked away to draw it off, Given regarded Pierson. "Sam couldn't send out the morning coach," he said.

Pierson looked him squarely in the eye as he replied, "Too damned bad."

Doughbelly brought the beer. Given pulled the glass close but made no attempt to raise it. He stood in thought for a moment then spoke to Pierson again. "Did you ever ride gun-guard?"

"Lots of times."

Given tasted the beer, which was tangy and tepid, put down the glass, and turned his head to belch discreetly before speaking again. "Care to do it again?"

Pierson studied the taller man impassively, flicked Doughbelly a wry look, and said, "For Sam? Not on your tintype. If he needs a gun-guard, let him do it himself."

Given snorted. "Sam? He can't see from me to you. Those glasses he wears got lenses as thick as the bottom of a whiskey bottle."

Doughbelly climbed back atop his stool. He was enjoying this although he couldn't for the life of him imagine why Sam Holt had sent Marshal Given to recruit Whit Pierson to ride gun-guard. Not after what had happened between them yesterday.

The lawman finished his beer, pushed the glass aside, and leaned on the counter, contemplating his eagle-beaked, slightly menacing face in the back-bar mirror. "It's not for Sam, it's for me." Noticing Doughbelly's unwavering stare, Given straightened up and jerked his head. "Come on outside. I want to explain something to you."

"Say it right here," Pierson replied, and Marshal Given wagged his head. "Walls got ears."

Pierson exchanged another wry look with Doughbelly before following Jack Given out of the saloon. Doughbelly got down off his stool, scooped up Given's glass, took it to the tub of washwater, sank it, and said, "Humph!"

Outside, there was less roadway and sidewalk traffic than there had been earlier. As Pierson stood with the marshal, Given put his attention upon a freight outfit being pulled into town from the north by eight Spanish mules. He continued to watch this outfit as he told Pierson about Bonner's offer, and his urgency about delivering two thousand dollars to the bank down at Livermore.

As the freighter ground past, Given lost interest in it and turned to look at Pierson. "I told him I'd drive the stage if Sam was agreeable."

Pierson was scowling. "Does Sam know there'll be two thousand dollars aboard?"

"I don't know. Charley will likely tell him."

"Naw, he won't, Jack. If Sam agrees for you to tool the stage, you better tell him exactly what you'll be hauling besides those three passengers."

"All right . . . Whit, let me put it this way. There's half a dozen men around town I could get to ride guard. I don't want any of them. Will you make the run with me?"

"I don't think so. I'm obliged that you'd ask me, though."

As Pierson walked southward toward the lower end of town, Marshal Given watched for a few moments, then turned to face across the road in the direction of the corralyard. As he was standing there, Charley Bonner emerged from Sam Holt's office and struck out for his bank without looking left or right.

Jack Given lifted his hat, scratched, reset the hat, and waited until Bonner had disappeared inside his brick building. He struck out for the corralyard.

3

Three Soiled Towels

WHEN Marshal Given entered the stage company office Sam Holt was wearing his green eyeshade and had the lighted coal-oil lamp on his desk. He looked up, regarded Given for a moment, then leaned back and said, "Charley wants you to herd Whit's southbound down to Livermore."

Given nodded, went to the chair near the stove, and sat down.

"And," Holt went on, "he's sending some money to the bank down there on the same stage." Holt held up a hand as though he expected an interruption, but since Marshal Given already knew all this, he said nothing. "He's agreed to pay for a gun-guard."

Given still said nothing.

Holt peered owlishly at him. "Did you agree to drive the coach, Jack?"

"Yes. For fifty dollars an' if he sends along a guard," stated the lawman, remembering what Pierson had said about the likelihood that Bonner would not tell Sam he was going to send money down yonder. Evidently Charley had indeed learned his lesson.

Holt removed his glasses, groped for a blue bandanna, and went to work vigorously polishing them. "You got a choice among the fellers who've rode shotgun for me."

"Whit Pierson."

Sam stopped polishing, squeezed his eyes nearly closed, and stared. "He's mad. He won't do it, and I'm not goin' to ask him to." Sam resumed his polishing. "How about Dan Crockett? I've used him many times."

Marshal Given watched Holt hook his glasses into place as he answered. "Is he sober?"

Holt grimaced. "Most likely he is. Hell, it's not noon yet. I'll send someone to find him. Jack, Charley'd like the stage to leave real soon, within the next hour, and to tell the truth, so would I. There's three folks hangin' around town madder'n wet hens because they figured they'd be on their way on Whit's stage this morning, early."

Marshal Given blew out a big breath and stood up. "Get the outfit ready."

"It's ready. All we got to do is round up them passengers, put the horses on the pole, and—"

"And make damned sure Crockett's sober."

"Yes, sure. Get something to eat an' meet me out back directly."

Given returned to the roadway. He knew the gun-guard named Crockett; in fact, the marshal had jailed him a few times to sober up. Except for his drinking, Crockett would be satisfactory so long as Given could not get Whit Pierson to go south with him.

He went down to the jailhouse, booted a Winchester, took his sheep-pelt-lined coat from its wall peg, and returned to the corralyard. He put the gun and coat in the boot below the driver's seat, then went over to the bank, where Charley Bonner met him with raised eyebrows. Given held out a hand. "Payment in advance. Sam's getting things together. You better sack up that money an' take it over there."

Bonner continued to gaze upward at the tall man in front of his desk. "How about the shotgun-rider?"

"Dan Crockett. Sam's goin' to corral him. I hope he's sober." He pushed the hand out a little farther. Bonner eyed it, scratched his neck, arose, and groped in a trouser pocket. He counted out the money as he placed the notes on Given's palm. When that was done he wagged his head but said nothing until he was seated again. "I'll send the money over. It will be in one of the bank's leather pouches. How soon will you leave?"

"Maybe less than an hour." Given paused at the door and said, "Charley, it might be a good idea if you was to explain to Doughbelly and Walt Coggins that I won't be around for a couple of days, so's they can get the town possemen to keep an eye on things." The marshal turned and left the bank.

Bonner watched him head for the roadway, then arose to go first to the general store and later up to the saloon. He told Coggins and Doughbelly Price that the marshal would be away a couple of days, but he didn't say why or where Given was going. Coggins and Doughbelly were both part of the Beaverton posse organization; they would pass word around town. On his way back to the bank, Bonner stopped in front of the gunsmith's shop to watch a faded, sturdy old coach trundle out of Holt's corralyard, make a very wide sweep to the right, and line out southward through town.

As the outfit passed, Jack Given put a bleak look in the banker's direction and barely nodded. Beside him Dan Crockett sat with a long-barreled rifle positioned in an upright position between his legs. Crockett's bearded, craggy face did not turn toward the men on the sidewalk. As Bonner was resuming his walk northward, his clerk met him with a report. He had pouched the money for the Livermore bank, double-counted it, and had taken it over to the corralyard, where he'd asked Sam Holt for a receipt. The clerk held up the paper for Bonner to see.

Doctor Muller was standing out front of the general store with Walt Coggins as the coach passed. He said, "That's Jack up there."

Coggins nodded. "An' Dan Crockett. Something's going on, Carl. Jack's supposed to be minding the town, not herding a stage for Sam. I think I'll go up there and find out what this is all about."

The doctor brought forth a fresh cigar, lighted it with

care, blew smoke, and chuckled. "Crockett's in trouble. He's not going to be able to stick his snoot in a bottle as long as he's with Jack."

The storekeeper was not interested in the gun-guard, so he did not comment as they stood watching the coach and four reach the lower end of Beaverton with an arrow-straight stretch of roadway dead ahead of them for many miles.

From behind the fly-specked window of the harness works, Whit Pierson saw the Livermore coach pass southward. Hart, too, paused at his sewing-horse to watch. When the stage was beyond sight he went back to patching a *rosadero* some cowboy's tomfool horse had ripped loose in a pitching fit. With his head lowered as he worked, Hart shot an occasional gaze at Pierson. Finally, he said, "Sam's hard up for drivers an' I'm surprised Jack'd do it."

Pierson turned from the window to watch his friend sew for a moment before speaking. "He's gettin' fifty dollars for the trip."

Hart's head snapped up. "Fifty dollars? Where's he goin'— China?"

"Livermore and back."

Hart studied his friend in strong silence, then grunted and went back to work. Pierson filled a grimy crockery cup with black coffee at the wood-stove, returned to the counter, and leaned with the cup in his hand, watching Hart use his awl and two needles. "You think there'd be need for a drayage business around here, Tom?" he asked.

The harness maker let his pair of threaded needles dangle, leaned with both arms across the high, curved jaws of the sewing horse, and studied his friend. "Maybe. You'd be competin' with Sam, and he's been doin' local hauling for a long time. Whit, I don't figure folks would favor you over Sam just because someone told 'em he done you a dirty trick. I got a better idea. I haven't been caught up in here for two years, haven't had time to go into the mountains fishing, an'

I know I'm gettin' a little mean from working ten hours a damned day seven days a damned week. Tell you what I'll do—sell you a partnership, share an' share alike, for two hunnert dollars."

Pierson tasted the coffee, which was more bitter than original sin, and put the cup down. "I don't know a damned thing about makin' saddles or harnesses, Tom. I've rode 'em and hitched up teams, but—"

"I didn't know anything, either, when I opened up here ten, twelve years back. I can show you what I know."

Pierson smiled at his old friend. "I'll think on it," he said, and headed for the doorway. He had almost reached it when Hart called to him. "Hey, that's a waste of coffee. You didn't finish it."

Pierson grinned. "That's one of the things I got to think about, Tom. Whether I could put up with your coffee for the rest of my life."

He crossed the road and was turning southward toward the lower end of town where he had his cottage, when a dark, pockmarked man emerged from the general store, carrying packages he could barely see over. The two men almost collided. Pierson said, "Pete, you need a wheelbarrow. What is all that stuff, new sheets and towels for the rooming house?"

Pete leaned to place his packages on a wall bench before replying. (He was the only Mexican in Beaverton. His name was Pedro, but everyone called him Pete.) He seemed willing to talk, and he was angry. "New sheets. Sixty-five cents for flannel. They slept with their boots on. Walt said I should be glad they weren't wearing spurs. They was only here over-night. It'll take me a month to make up what I lost on 'em."

"Who? Those passengers off my coach who had to lie over until today to go on south?"

"Yes. Cigar burns in their rooms, torn sheets, and spilt whiskey where they played cards in one of the rooms almost all night. Like pigs. Worse than pigs."

Pierson got a furrow across his forehead. "Cigar burns in their rooms?"

"All three rooms, yes. Come with me. I'll show you how they burned the dressers, the windowsills. Now I got to sand the burns down and repaint everything."

"Pete, all three rooms?"

"I just told you. Yes, all three rooms."

"You had other customers?"

"No. Just them three. I haven't had much trade since early spring." Pete glared at the packages as though his trouble could be attributed to them. "I was glad when they come along, maybe business was going to pick up now."

"Two men and a woman?" Pierson asked, trying to be sure he and Pete were talking about the same people.

The Mexican faced him, still looking venomous. "Yes."

"Did you see the woman smoking a cigar, Pete?"

"No. But she smoked them. Come with me and I'll show you her room. And the sheets where she slept with her boots on."

Pierson helped Pete carry the packages and started northward, wearing a puzzled, worried expression.

At the rooming house they left the packages in the parlor while Pete showed him the rooms. Exactly as Pete had said, there were stogie scars in all three rooms. Most of them appeared to be in the room the Mexican said the woman had paid for.

Soiled, stained flannel sheets had been stripped from the bed and piled into a corner. Pete crossed over to hold up a soiled sheet for Pierson to examine. "Mud," he exclaimed. "Adobe-mud stain don't come out. I know. I can boil these sheets until they fall apart and the brown stain will still be there."

Pierson's gaze slid from the ruined sheet to the other pieces of cloth in the corner. He moved past the Mexican to disentangle a worn towel and scowled at it. He took it to the only window in the room and held it to the light. As he lowered it, he faced Pete. "Let's see the other sheets and towels."

The Mexican was glad to lead the way. He had tried to denounce his recent roomers to Coggins at the general store, but Coggins had other customers and commiserated only very briefly before walking away.

In each room Pierson pawed through the discarded articles until he found towels. In each case he took the towels to a window to verify what had surprised him in the woman's room. Men had shaved. They had probably done as most men did who used straight razors; they had draped a towel over one shoulder and after each swipe down a lathered cheek, had wiped the blade on the towel.

Pete sensed something. He watched everything Pierson did, as it eventually dawned on him that men had shaved in each of the three rooms. His eyes got very round as he said, "*Compadre* . . . she was a he?"

Pierson tossed a towel aside. "Unless she was a bearded lady. I saw one once in a circus over in Denver, only the feller I was with said it wasn' really her hair, it was just stuck on her face. But not this time, Pete. This time it was real hair and . . ."

"What are you staring at?"

"Why would a man dress up like a woman?"

Pete shrugged thick shoulders. "Who knows? Maybe she was hiding from the law. I mean, maybe he was an outlaw and—"

Pierson was moving past in the direction of the hallway as he said, "Oh hell."

He left the rooming house with Pete trailing as far as the dilapidated old front porch. Out there, Pete sank into a rickety chair and watched Pierson. He was almost trotting by the time he reached the corralyard, where he turned in, leaving the Mexican still sitting on his porch.

4

Some Bad Thoughts

SAM Holt's weak and watery eyes popped wide open when Whit Pierson burst into his corralyard office. The longer he listened to Pierson, the less relevance their personal feud appeared to have. When Pierson had finished his story, Holt got up from behind his desk, looked around for the hat he crushed atop his head, and said, "Come on. Charley's got to hear this."

But the banker was not at his desk. A clerk told them he was at the café. They hurried down there, were told Bonner was across the road at the leather works, and arrived in Tom Hart's doorway half-breathless.

Holt started speaking in a shrill voice, running his words together, until Tom Hart yelled at him in disgust. "Calm down. Just shut up for a minute, Sam. You're not makin' any sense."

Pierson spoke without taking his eyes off the banker, whose face was becoming progressively pale. When Pierson had finished Charley stepped to the counter and leaned on it.

Hart moved to his cutting table and perched there as he said, "Well, if that's what they're planning, them boys might get a surprise. Jack's no greenhorn."

The other three men looked steadily at Hart, who shifted slightly in his chair. Pierson said, "They are *under* him. They are *inside* the coach. Jack's up there on the seat, him and

Crockett. Those three can get the drop anywhere along the road Jack stops to water or blow the horses."

Hart made a final effort to appease the agitation of his friends. "It don't have to mean they're after the pouch. They wouldn't know about it, anyway. Most likely, if they're outlaws, an' one of 'em is dressed up like a woman, all they want is to get a hell of a long way from somewhere up north."

Pierson, who'd had more time to consider things, looked at Charley Bonner. "One thing is a damned fact. If they're outlaws an' decided to rob the coach, Jack and Crockett are likely to end up dead beside the road. . . . But it sticks in my mind that they rode my coach down here to Beaverton an' I was carryin' the money."

Hart seized on that. "Sure. There you are. If they'd been highwaymen they'd have stopped Whit and robbed his coach. They'd have got Charley's money."

"They couldn't have known the money was on Whit's coach," stated the banker.

Pierson shrugged at that. "Charley, your damned money is on Jack's coach. That's what matters. Not what happened before."

"It's not my money. It belongs to the Livermore bank, and I got a receipt from Sam that it was handed over to him to deliver down there."

Pierson was annoyed. "Forget who's responsible for a minute. As far as I'm concerned the money don't matter. I'm worried about Jack and Crockett. Sure as we're standin' around here when we should be ahorseback, Given an' Crockett are ridin' along watchin' both sides and up ahead, an' they got three men inside their coach who could damned well be outlaws."

Hart slid off his worktable, scowled at Holt and Bonner, took down his old shellbelt and holstered sidearm, and went to work buckling the belt around his lean middle. "Somebody get Doughbelly an' Doc Muller. Charley, get your coat an' weapons and meet us down at the livery barn."

Holt reacted to this abrupt activity by announcing that he too would get rigged out to ride and meet the others at the lower end of town. Holt was the first to leave the harness shop. The other three hung back. No one showed any enthusiasm. As part of the Beaverton posse organization they had been on other manhunts with Sam Holt. When the shooting started, he had proved himself to be more of a peril to his friends than to his enemies.

The banker departed, leaving Hart and Pierson behind. As Hart settled his holstered six-gun he squinted at Pierson. "If this turns out to be a wild goose chase . . ." He wagged his head and said no more as he looked around for the padlock to his front door.

Whit Pierson was worrying by the time he got down to his cottage behind the town smithy. Even if that "woman" was indeed a man, which Whit was absolutely convinced of, he/she did not have to be an outlaw. Maybe he was a man who liked to dress like women. Whit had never heard of such a thing, but years earlier he had been told of a woman who had dressed as a Confederate soldier and had gone through several battles before being wounded, at which time her secret was revealed at a field hospital. Sometimes there just was no accounting for folks.

But the oddness of the "woman" was not what troubled him. He had aroused a number of people with the allegation that the "woman" and her two male companions were probably high-tailing-it outlaws. Nothing more, actually, than an idea that had popped into his mind because the stage they were riding on was carrying a money pouch—about which they had no inkling. Or did they?

He locked his house and went over to the livery barn with a booted Winchester over his shoulder and a belt gun cinched around his middle.

The others were already there, and the livery-barn dayman was rushing around like a chicken with its head off, bringing in animals, dragging saddlery from the harness room, and worrying himself sick because his employer was gone for the day and all the responsibility was his and for fifty years he had been avoiding responsibility. Any kind at all. Nor could he elicit explanations from the possemen about why they were all bristling with armament, where they were going, and when they might return the horses, things his employer would want to know.

When they led the animals out front to be turned a couple of times, then mounted, the dayman leaned in a wide doorway, watching and sweating. As the riders turned southward on the stage road, he saw only in which direction they were riding before rushing up to the saloon where Doughbelly's substitute beamed from behind the bar.

It was a warm, pleasant day, the air was like glass, and visibility was limited only by distant upthrusts. On both sides of the roadbed the country had been burned over so many times there were few trees, and they were some distance off.

The possemen were impressed by the fact that with all this perfect visibility they did not see Marshal Given's coach up ahead where the road ran arrow-straight toward a notch in some distant, forested hills.

Tom Hart took the dissenting advocate's role again as he waved a long arm. "He's been gone from town about three, maybe four hours." Tom dropped his arm and squinted at Pierson, the only man among them who had driven stages over this route many times. "Would he still be in sight, Whit?"

Pierson answered dryly. "See how straight that road is, Tom? Runs about ten, maybe fifteen miles dead ahead toward that notch. It's called In'ian Gap. A driver can cover quite a few miles with a loaded coach in maybe three, four hours, but he can't cover any fifteen miles in that time. Do you see any stage up there? I don't."

Walt Coggins spoke around a chewing-cigar and from beneath a shapeless old hat. "Kick 'em out, Tom. Pick up the gait. Poking along like this is going to make me late for supper this evening, an' Missus Coggins don't take kindly to that. That coach left the road."

Sam Holt had his hat pulled so low to protect his eyes he had to squint upward to see from beneath the brim. At mention of his coach having left the roadbed he groaned loudly. Tom Hart looked back at him. "Maybe he went out to water the horses, Sam. Maybe somethin' else."

Holt seemed not to have heard. He rode leaning forward, watching the roadbed, until Doughbelly eased up to ride stirrup with him and offered a bottle. Sam took two grateful swallows, muttered his gratitude, and went back to watching tracks.

Whit was rhythmically chewing when the harness maker up ahead leaned from the saddle on the left side and called out. "Ahead. Up ahead the wheel tracks go out yonder." He straightened in the saddle to point.

They reined off the coach road, following Tom Hart and only occasionally glancing at the well-defined tracks they were following.

They were crossing rangeland covered with springtime grass up to a man's stirrups. There were some scattered trees a fair distance eastward. Southeastward the stands of timber were thicker; they made a distant eastward curve and bent around southward until they met the timbered slopes of the distant hills.

As Pierson rode along he was beginning to feel seriously worried. Whips did not leave roadways with passengers on a stage, unless there was a very good reason. Like perhaps three cocked pistols to persuade them to depart from their route and schedule.

Sam Holt fidgeted with his scraggly dragoon mustache and peered ahead as he rode. Whether the money pouch was lost or not, and whether he would be responsible for its loss, bothered him less than the loss of the four horses on the pole of his missing stagecoach, and the coach itself.

Doctor Muller—a thick, burly man of indeterminate years

who wore matching britches and coat in summer and winter, sometimes with a city-type necktie—rode tieless now. He said very little unless he was spoken to, but his keen eyes blocked in squares of the onward countryside for methodical examination. He left the sign reading to Tom Hart. Doctor Muller's interest was in the stands of trees they were approaching. As a former wartime surgeon, he knew what men looked like after they had been ambushed.

Doughbelly, with a bottle in each saddle pocket, was beginning to ache from the ride. He was unaccustomed to this sort of travel, and even in his earlier years when a saddle animal had been almost the only method of transportation between two points, he had never enjoyed saddlebacking. For one thing, he was not built for it. For another thing, as a result of several unpleasant encounters as a youngster, Doughbelly had never got over his distrust of horses.

But it was Doughbelly Price—not Tom Hart, who was riding in the lead—who saw something about a mile ahead that made him call ahead to Hart. "Tom—southward on your right. Do you see that break in the land?"

They all turned to locate evidence of an arroyo and were still looking down there when the wheel marks turned abruptly in that direction.

Hart held up a hand, slackened his reins, and sat in silence for a moment, scanning the countryside. When the others clustered around him, he eased his weight slightly in the saddle as he said, "Rest your behinds. I'll see what's over there."

No one urged a mount to follow the harness maker. Pierson jettisoned his cud, spat, and swung off to stand at his horse's head. The others did the same. The animals got as much slack in the reins as they could and began to crop grass disinterestedly.

Hart appeared about half-size to them by the time he pulled down to a slow walk to approach the arroyo. They saw him halt and sit for a long time like a statue, before urging his animal closer. He stopped again, this time about six feet from the lip of the gully.

He stood in his stirrups and wigwagged with his hat. The watchers mounted and rode ahead in absolute silence, eyes fixed on the harness maker, who was sitting too straight, telegraphing alarm by his immobility.

They were about fifty feet behind when Hart turned and spoke without raising his voice. "It's down there. Doc, there's an arm an' a leg visible on the far side. Looks like the rest of him is under the coach."

They halted, swung down, looked for things to tie the horses to, and went up to the edge of the arroyo. It was fairly deep, the result, no doubt, of centuries of rainfall runoff following the line of least resistance, a little swale, and making the swale deeper and wider until the arroyo came into existence.

The stagecoach was half on its side, half on its top as though it had been pushed or levered over the rim, not as though it had been driven over it.

Carl Muller led the way down, crumbly soil breaking away underfoot, until he reached the bottom on the seat of his britches.

Sam Holt was looking southward to where the arroyo made a crooked bend beyond which it was not possible to see from the locale of the overturned stagecoach. He was seeking shod-horse tracks, but if there were any, they were hidden by stands of thick, spiny, heatherlike undergrowth.

He went over to look at his coach, but had his attention pulled elsewhere when a deep voice said, "Find some poles to prise it off him with."

Doughbelly arose from a squatting position as he said, "He's dead, Carl. Squashed flat."

Doctor Muller's temper flared. "Just get him out from under there, damn it!"

Pierson and Hart searched for fifteen minutes before locating anything suitable. Doughbelly and Sam Holt were more fortunate. They took the two pieces of seasoned ash that had been the tongue of the coach, got them in place with round rocks back a few feet, and were red in the face from straining by the time Hart and Pierson returned. With four pry-bars and twice as much muscle, the coach was hoisted about ten inches off the ground. Muller pulled Crockett from beneath the coach, and while his companions eased the rig back down, he knelt to make an examination, with Sam Holt looking over his shoulder.

The other men were breathing hard and sweating. The coach was not especially heavy, but the way it was canted against the side of the arroyo made lifting it about as easy as prying up a building.

Pierson went over to stand beside Sam Holt as Doctor Muller completed his examination, covered the corpse with its coat, and stood up. Holt removed his glasses to polish them as he said, "It rarely happens like that. When a coach goes over it flings 'em clear, even if they don't have the time to jump, which they usually do have."

Muller's retort was curt. "Not this time. Crockett didn't have time to jump." Muller watched Holt resetting his glasses. "He was dead before the stagecoach went over the edge."

Sam's eyes, magnified by the lenses of his glasses, looked huge. Doctor Muller gazed at the covered body at his feet. "Shot from behind. He landed on his back, the coach landed on top of his chest and belly. But in back where things weren't all broken apart, he's got a bullet hole between his shoulderblades. The slug probably came out in front, but there's no way to be sure of that, the way he got squashed."

Muller blew out a ragged breath and looked at his companions. They were not looking at him but at the body covered by a rough old drover's coat.

Doughbelly eventually said, "Where's Marshal Given?"

They scattered out to look. They did not find another body. They did not even find any boot tracks, although they diligently searched the arroyo.

They did not find a money pouch either, but as Tom Hart and Whit Pierson worked their way through the dense, thorny southward underbrush, down where the arroyo made a dogleg bend, they found a blue gingham dress, a wig of long, wavy brown hair hanging on a willow limb, and two shellbelts with holstered Colts.

They sang out for the others and pressed their search. The last thing they located down there was a shotgun that someone had struck violently against something hard enough to shatter the wooden stock and the cocking mechanism.

Whit used a narrow little game trail to get back up out of the arroyo. He paused up there to tongue a fresh cud of molasses-cured into his cheek, then quartered slowly, searching for tracks.

He found them without difficulty. The horses had been taken off the stage before the coach was shoved over the rim of the arroyo. Whit was returning from tracking the horseshoe-sign when his companions straggled up from the deep place.

Sam Holt looked at him. "What'd you find?"

Whit forced a small smile at Holt. "You always said you would buy only combination horses, Sam."

"Yeah."

"There's your reward," said Pierson, gesturing to shod-horse marks leading away from the arroyo. "If you'd bought harness horses broke to pull instead of combination horses broke to ride as well as pull, those murderers wouldn't have got away as clean as they did. . . . Sam, you better go back for a wagon to haul Crockett back in, an' bring your yardmen an' some tools to get that coach rightside up and out of there."

Pierson turned toward the other possemen. "We still got a lot of daylight . . . but if we sight them, I have a hunch it'll be the beginnin' of our trouble. They didn't take Marshal Given along because they was charmed by him."

5

A Hard Ride

SAM Holt loped in the direction of town and the others began their tracking. Tom Hart, the only one among them who had ever done much sign reading, took the lead, but Whit Pierson was troubled by the openness of the country as they worked back toward the stage road and crossed it, traveling westerly where there was no worthwhile cover, so he sashayed southward a fair distance to scout ahead while keeping the others in sight.

His disadvantage was that although he had lived in Beaverton for more than ten years and had made a few forays roundabout, he really did not know this southwesterly country at all. He tried consoling himself with the probability that the killers of Dan Crockett probably did not know it either, but that was not much consolation in an area where mounted men could see for miles when visibility was as good as it was today.

He halted once and sat with dangling reins, watching the others about a mile north of him. His horse ducked its head to snatch grass heads. Whit groped for his plug and gnawed off a corner. The nearest stand of trees was about two miles northwest, otherwise there was underbrush in scattered clumps, too short to conceal a horse but exactly the right height and density to hide bushwhackers. He spat, speculated about the route of the fleeing outlaws and, using Tom's course as a gauge, decided it was likely the outlaws had reached those distant trees several hours earlier. They were now probably well beyond them, riding in the direction of some blue-blurred distant mountains.

He was mindful of the possibility of being ambushed but thought it more likely that the outlaws' first concern would be to travel as far and as fast as they could.

He picked up the reins, watching the distant trees. They could be an advantage to the pursuers if the fleeing men were far enough west of them to be unable to see back where Whit and his companions were.

A ways off to Whit's right, Hart had halted. He and Doughbelly, the doctor, and the banker huddled, looking at something on the ground. Whit was curious but not sufficiently so to ride up there, and since they did not call or signal for him to join them, he kept on riding toward the line of distant timber.

The day had warmed up considerably the past couple of hours, and as heat usually did, it lowered and blurred visibility.

Whit slackened to a slow walk when he was within rifle-range of the timber. He watched closely for any kind of movement and found none. He rode within carbine range and finally halted to watch his companions ride up and do the same thing. He signaled for them to stay where they were, eased his animal into an easy lope, and leaned on his approach to the timber to lift his carbine from its saddleboot and ride with it balanced across his lap.

Nothing happened. He reached fragrant pine shade, dropped to a walk, and made his way among big old trees of which most seemed to be overripe and deteriorating, as he angled northward seeking tracks.

When he eventually found them his friends arrived. They dismounted where there had been a hasty rest-halt and studied the sign. It was impossible to determine which boot tracks belonged to Marshal Given.

Doughbelly came up and opened a closed fist. He was holding Marshal Given's nickel badge on his palm. "I'd have figured he'd have found a way to get rid of it before he come this far, wouldn't you?"

Both Coggins and Pierson stared at the badge. Coggins said, "They don't know they took a lawman prisoner?"

"Jack might not have got this far if they'd known earlier," Tom Hart said, walking up and standing hip-shot, thumbs hooked in his old shellbelt. Tom looked westward. "There's a cow outfit against the foothills over yonder. Belongs to a cranky old cuss named Flaherty. I went huntin' over there one time an' he run me off." Hart faced forward eyeing his companions. "Those boys been pretty hard on Sam's horses. If they expect to keep on like they been doing, they got to get fresh saddlestock." Tom smiled without a shred of humor. "That's the only place they're goin' to find 'em, an' if they aren't careful that old man'll skin 'em alive."

Whit gazed out through the trees to more open country. "They aren't the only ones that'll need fresh horses, Tom."

Doughbelly pocketed Jack Given's badge and started over toward his horse. The others followed. From this point on, Whit remained with his companions. The moment they broke clear of the trees, heat hit them. They had no cover from this point all the way to the distant foothills, not even any worthwhile brush. The reason for this was basic to the kind of country on ahead and on both sides for many miles: cattlemen kept timber and brush off their grasslands by setting the land afire after moving their cattle somewhere else. Over the years the desired result was achieved; neither trees nor brush interfered with the growth of grass.

"They've seen us by now, sure as hell," Coggins offered, looking dead ahead where rolling foothill country yielded westerly to a rising, rugged backdrop of heavily timbered uplands. No one disputed this, not even Tom, who seemed to have a knack of trying to mitigate what anyone else said. He rode slouched and pensive, watching for rooftops, which eventually came into view, backgrounded by the darkly timbered mountains. He raised an arm as he said, "That there low log building with the sod roof is the main house." He lowered his arm, eyeing the massive, functionally ugly residence. "I don't know whether Flaherty's got riders or not. Most likely he has. I saw a lot of cattle and horses that time I rode over here, too much livestock for a one-man ranch."

They rode another hundred yards before Doughbelly made an observation. "Seems awful quiet to me. No smoke from the chimney, no one around the corrals or the yard. You don't suppose . . .?"

The harness maker scowled. "Naw. We'd have heard the shooting."

Doughbelly remained unconvinced. "It's too quiet, Tom."

They rode to within a mile and halted. Doughbelly was correct, there was no sign of life in the yard. Doctor Muller urged his horse forward. The others followed his example. They had almost reached the yard when a distant shout made them stop again and twist to find the source of the yell.

Three riders were approaching at a lope. Two of the horsemen were larger than the man in the middle, who seemed to be little more than sinew, bone, and hide. Tom Hart said, "That's Flaherty, the one in the middle."

When the strangers were closer they dropped to a steady walk as the two groups studied each other. Carl Muller edged slightly ahead, and when the strangers halted he looked straight at the bleak-eyed older man in front of him. "We're from Beaverton," he said, speaking firmly, permitting no interruption. "Three outlaws made off with a money pouch from a coach going down to Livermore, killed the gun-guard, dumped the stage in a gully, and rode in this direction on the harness horses. They took the driver with them. He's Jack Given, town marshal of Beaverton."

The wizened cowman stared at Doctor Muller. His two riders did too, but their expressions reflected shock, not testiness. Muller introduced himself, pointed to his companions as he named each one, then rested both hands atop the saddlehorn and waited.

The cowman studied Tom, Whit, and Doughbelly. When he looked at the harness maker his eyes perceptibly narrowed, but when he spoke he addressed Muller. "You're the doctor from Beaverton?"

Carl nodded.

The old man seemed to loosen a little. "Well now, ain't that an act of Providence? Doctor, I got this itchin' in the legs an' there ain't no rash or—"

Muller looked from his greater height down his nose at the cowman. "We just introduced ouselves," he said. "We may be a long distance from town, but even out here I'd expect folks to be concerned about a murder."

The riders looked swiftly at the cowman, whose pale eyes became unwaveringly fixed on Carl Muller. "Name's Mike Flaherty," he said, biting the words off. "This here on my left is Tighe Butler. This gent on my right is Bill Greenleaf. That satisfy you, Doctor?"

Whit did not dare glance at Tom Hart. He might smile, and he was sure old Flaherty would notice. Whit had never seen Carl Muller yank the slack out of anyone before. It surprised him because in all the years he had known the doctor, Muller had always been good-natured, pleasant to be around, and seemingly easygoing.

Carl did not say whether the belated introductions had satisfied him or not. He instead asked a question. "Have you seen four men riding big combination horses? They're riding bareback and they came due west from beyond those trees back a few miles. Their tracks—"

"Their tracks," old Flaherty interrupted, "didn't come this far west. They likely didn't know the country, and when they seen our buildings, they cut off back the way they'd come, makin' for them trees. That's where we been. Tighe seen four riders coming. When they suddenly turned back he raised the yell, and the three of us went out lookin' for them."

"Did you see them?"

"No. Only from a distance. They slid back into the timber before we could reach 'em."

"May be just as well," opined Doughbelly. "They'd have bushwhacked you."

Old Flaherty smiled at Doughbelly as he said quietly, "Mister, I been out here forty years—there was sneakin' redskins back then. They're gone but I ain't. Been lots of horsethieves and cowthieves and whatnot pass through. They're gone too, an' I'm still here. I can smell a bushwhack a mile off."

Doughbelly did not open his mouth again, but Whit did. "Mister Flaherty, they got to get fresh horses. They've rode those stage animals about into the ground. Do you have loose stock in the direction they rode?"

Flaherty shook his head. "Not northward. Aren't supposed to be northward anyway. We been turnin' cattle back from the mountains for the last three, four days, so I ain't sure exactly where our loose stock is, but it's usually south, down toward the hot-spring sump."

Whit gazed from one of the old man's riders to the other one; they returned his look with expressionless faces. Neither of them said a word until Walt Coggins asked Flaherty if he and his companions could get fresh saddlestock, then the man named Greenleaf wagged his head as he replied, "We don't have no extra horses caught up. We was goin' to do that in a few days, but right now all we got is what we're settin' on and some barefoot colts at the corrals."

Flaherty nodded his head all the while his rider was speaking. He grinned at Carl Muller. "You're up a creek without a paddle, Doctor. Those gents will be widenin' the gap while we're settin' here jawboning. If I was you gents and wanted to catch some renegades, I'd be crowdin' them somethin' fierce instead of wastin' time."

Flaherty's perpetually narrowed eyes drifted to Tom Hart. He'd seemed to be struggling with something earlier. Evidently he had found it because he said, "Been a while since I met you. Last time I told you not to come back. You remember that?"

Tom remembered and he was not daunted. "I remember just like it was yesterday, you cranky old goat. If you was twenty years younger I'd haul you off that horse and stomp you a little."

Whit held his breath. So did Doughbelly, but the banker leaned on the saddlehorn and addressed old Flaherty. "Some other time, maybe. Don't get off that horse, Mister Flaherty. He'll do it, and we're in kind of a hurry. Some other time. Maybe you'll come to Beaverton. I'm president of the bank there. If I can't get your attention, Doctor Muller can. It's been my experience that everyone comes to one or the other of us sometime in his life."

Muller turned his horse. Bonner and Coggins followed. Whit jerked his head at Hart, who was glowering, rode his horse over, and nudged Hart's animal. Doughbelly brought up the rear, looking over his shoulder with a sickly little smile.

They had covered about half the distance toward the timber they had passed through earlier when a small band of loose horses burst out of the speckled tree shadows, running toward them. When they were close enough to see mounted men, they veered wildly southward.

Everyone halted to watch. Far back someone yelled. Old Flaherty and his riders were fanning out to funnel the loose stock into some pole corrals. Charley Bonner brightened. "Fresh horses," he exclaimed hopefully, and got a brusque retort from Doctor Muller. "It'd be a waste of time, Charley. He wouldn't let us have any if his life depended on it. Let's go."

Whit called out. He had been watching the loose animals closely. As his companions turned, he pointed to the drag where the slowest horses were not quite able to keep up. "Harness horses," he exclaimed. "Four of them."

Tom Hart squeezed his eyes nearly closed in an effort to see the horses better. He was unsure if Whit was right, but he was perfectly willing to ride back and find out. As he was reining around he said, "They sure as hell didn't set them harness horses loose until they'd caught fresh animals, an' that puts a different light on things. Carl, you run a good bluff on that old goat. . . . Let's go back an' see if you can do it again, because sure as gawd made little green apples, we got to have fresh horses too—or we can forget about catchin' those bastards."

No one said a word as they turned to follow Tom back toward old Flaherty's yard, where dust was rising around the network of working corrals.

6

Toward Sunset

FLAHERTY and his two riders had been fully occupied making sure the loose stock went through a large pole gateway, and afterward they had stood in rank dust with their backs to the westerly country, examining what they had corralled. They saw the worn-down combination horses with a strange mark on their left shoulders and had a lengthy discussion about this, then turned to put up their riding stock—and saw the riders from Beaverton returning.

They finished caring for their animals and went to lean out front of the log barn against a long tie-rack, waiting. Neither of the old cowman's riders said a word; whatever came of this second meeting would be up to their employer. They would back him, whatever it was.

Doctor Muller was in the lead, with Whit Pierson on his left side, when they crossed the yard and halted a few yards from the waiting stockmen. Carl looked steadily at Flaherty, who looked just as steadily back. Muller cleared his throat and Flaherty said, "I told you gents—if you want to catch renegades, you got to push 'em something fierce."

Doctor Muller replied curtly. "Mister Flaherty, I never rode a horse to death in my life and I'm too old to change now." Muller jutted his jaw in the direction of the dusty corrals, like an Indian. "We need fresh animals."

Both Flaherty's riders had been standing with arms crossed over their chests. At Muller's words, and the hard way they had been spoken, Greenleaf and Butler slowly

40

unfolded their arms and let them hang. They were watching Muller, Whit, and Hart, who was on Muller's off-side. Flaherty was watching them, too, when a slightly unsteady voice spoke from farther back. Doughbelly Price was holding an uncocked six-gun in his right hand, thumb poised on the hammer.

Having been partially concealed by the men in front of him, he had been able to draw the gun and aim it. He said, "Hate to do this, gents, but like you said, Mister Flaherty, we got to push those outlaws somethin' fierce. Now then, reach across with your left hands, lift out them pistols, and drop them. Real careful."

Doughbelly cocked his handgun. That little sound was very loud in the utter silence. The banker, who was about six feet away on Doughbelly's left side, eyed the saloonman for a moment, then drew his weapon, too, urged his horse ahead, and cocked it.

Mike Flaherty's pale eyes moved in little fits and starts right up until Walt Coggins eased up and cocked his gun, too, then the old cowman leaned, spat, straightened back, and grinned from ear to ear. Without taking his eyes off the men from Beaverton he spoke to his riders. "You lads go cut out the best horses. One for each of these gents and one for me. Fetch 'em around here where we can saddle up. I'll ride with 'em. You boys stay home and finish lookin' for cattle up in the trees."

As Butler and Greenleaf turned without a word to go down through the log barn in the direction of the corrals out back, Flaherty looked at Doughbelly. "Mister, what do you do for a living?"

"Run a saloon up in Beaverton."

Flaherty nodded as though this confirmed something for him. "What's your name? I forgot."

"Price. Frank Price, but folks call me Doughbelly."

Flaherty's faded eyes twinkled. "Be careful when you ease that hammer down, Doughbelly, an' put up the gun. You didn't buffalo me. I never been shot at by a barman yet, an' I could tell you wasn't used to guns when you was talkin', and I might have taken a chance on you missin' except for one thing—those dirty, skulkin' whelps you're after stole four of my saddle horses, and partner, no one's ever done that an' lived to brag about it. Not in over forty years. Now then, get down gents, peel off your outfits, and I'll get my rig." Flaherty turned to enter his barn. The banker watched him as he spoke from the side of his mouth to Doctor Muller. "Suppose he's got a gun in the barn."

Instead of answering, Muller swung heavily from the saddle and turned his back, then lifted the stirrup-leather to get at the latigo and cinch.

Whit did the same. They all did: dumped their outfits on the ground and were ready to resaddle when Flaherty's pair of poker-faced hired riders led out fresh animals.

While the resaddling was in progress, Mike Flaherty led his saddled animal out and halted to buckle a carbine boot under his right *rosadero*. Later, as he was swinging up across leather, he said, "Tighe, you boys finish ridin' the timber. If I ain't back by morning, go hunt up the rest of our loose stock and make a count. I don't expect any more will be missin', but I'd like to be sure." His little, faded blue eyes were pitiless. "If any more horses are gone, look for tracks, an' when I get back we'll do a little renegade huntin' of our own."

The Beaverton possemen heard this, saw the look on Flaherty's face, and when the old cowman turned to lead off out of the yard, Whit nudged Tom Hart and said softly, "That is a bloodthirsty old man if I ever saw one."

Hart looked down his hooked nose with its flaring nostrils and replied gruffly, "You think there's something wrong with that?"

With fresh animals under them and a man out front who knew this far-country better than he knew the back of his hand, the Beaverton riders made excellent time getting back to where they could pick up shod-horse marks. But Flaherty did not seek tracks among the trees, which Whit and Tom would have done; he picked up the gait riding parallel to the timber heading northward. Later, when they paused to blow the animals, he gestured impatiently and said, "Ain't no point in goin' out through the timber to where they caught my loose stock." He dropped his arm and squinted at his companions. "You boys probably hunted men before, but I've been doin' it before most of you was born, so let me explain somethin' to you. If you track men, you will always be behind them. You understand? You'll always be where they *been*, not where they *are*." He gestured again. "Those horsethieves went north. They lost some time sneakin' up on my loose stock, catchin' em, riggin' out, and headin' north again. Well, from now on we ain't goin' to waste any time. Let's go."

Doctor Muller was riding stirrup with Walt Coggins. As they loped ahead he frowned at old Flaherty's back and finally said, "Maybe they didn't keep riding northward. If I was in their boots I sure wouldn't have. Northward is where they came from—up in the Beaverton country. I'd go in any direction but that one."

The banker did not respond. He was as baffled as his friend was by the old cowman's action, but Flaherty had impressed him so he said nothing, just rode in Flaherty's wake and hoped Carl Muller was wrong.

He was, but they had a lowering sun off to their left before Flaherty swung to his right into the trees and, after a short lope, emerged into open country to the west. He halted, sitting like an Indian, hands at rest atop the saddlehorn, body motionless, eyes searching the land for movement. When he finally relaxed he said, "See any dust?"

The doctor shook his head without replying. Charley Bonner said, "No." He was standing in his stirrups when he spoke, not to see better but because his rear end was sore.

Pierson and Hart waited for movement, any kind at all, in

the sun-bright distance. Doughbelly kneed his animal up to them and pointed. "What's that? Ahead an' a little easterly. Ain't that dust?"

Old Flaherty turned in the saddle, wearing a wolfish grin. "Pussgut, come on up here an' ride with me." He waited as the saloonman urged his horse ahead, studying Doughbelly. When they were side by side Flaherty sat forward, raised his rein hand, and said, "In all my years I never before seen a saloonman who could see beyond the nearest bottle. Stay up here with me. That's dust for a damned fact, an' deer or cattle didn't make it." He shot a sidelong glance in the direction of the lowering sun and kneed his horse into motion, but now he eased back close to the trees as he struck out in another loose lope. He rode in silence, watching the far country without saying a word. Doughbelly rode with him, also looking up ahead. Behind them the others followed. Whit and Tom looked amused. The banker and doctor looked grim. That old scarecrow in the lead rode like he'd never done anything else and wasn't interested in the welfare of those riding with him. He probably had calluses on his butt as thick as bootsoles.

Shortly before dusk Flaherty slackened to a dogged walk and craned around to see how the men behind him were faring. He ignored Whit and the harness maker, looked longest at Charley and Carl, then spat and said, "We'll quit directly, an' you gents can find some nice soft pine needles to set on."

The banker reddened, but if being patronized bothered Doctor Muller, he showed no sign of it.

Doughbelly dug out his bottle, offered it to Flaherty, who looked more pleased than surprised, and after drinking from it passed it back to Muller. As the bottle went around, Flaherty looked intently at the saloonman. "I never cultivated folks," he stated. "Damned seldom anyway. You know what a misanthrope is, Pussgut?"

"Doughbelly—an' no, I never heard the word before, that I recollect."

"Excuse me. Doughbelly. I never was good at names. About twenty years back a preacher come through in a wagon. Him an' his wife. He was sickly so they stayed for a while, until he should have got better, only he didn't. He upped and died one night. Well, Doughbelly, one time him an' I was settin' in the shade, drinkin' a little, while his wife rassled supper in the house an' he told me I was a misanthrope.

"You know how it is when a man's been drinking. I lifted out my gun to shoot the son of a bitch. He begun to sweat an' told me a misanthrope is somebody who don't like people."

"What did you do?"

"Put up the gun, refilled his glass, and agreed with him. Now then, you're an exception. You not only got good eyes, ain't afraid to cock your gun at someone, but by gawd you can produce a bottle when a man's got such a thirst it's a downright misery to him." Old Flaherty struck Doughbelly roughly on the shoulder, looked around to see if the bottle was returning, and when Tom Hart handed it to him, he took one big swallow, passed it back to the saloonman, belched wetly, and said, "Banker, you know what we're doin' right now?"

Charley eyed Flaherty askance. "Drinking whiskey," he said.

Flaherty belched again before replying. "Yeah. But the reason we're doin' it right here, you see, is because from here until the sun goes down, those boys up yonder ridin' my horses can see dust. After sundown they can't."

Whit eyed the old man. "I'm curious about something," he said.

Flaherty made an expansive gesture. The whiskey was doing its work. "All right. Fire away."

"What became of the preacher's wife?"

For a full thirty seconds old Flaherty rode along studying the dying day, the bronzelike heavens, as though he had not heard Whit's question, or as though Whit had not asked it. He dropped his gaze to his horse's moving ears.

"She stayed," he finally said, and glanced into tree shadows on his left side. "Her name was Marianne. That's a pretty name, ain't it? Marianne. She was pretty as a dogwood tree in full bloom. She laughed a lot, too. She stayed a spell. In them days Livermore wasn't more'n a way station with a peach tree beside the road. We went down there, found a preacher, and got married. Then we drove the wagon back. . . . She died that autumn. Doughbelly, anything left in that bottle?"

There was. Not much, but enough. For a long time no one spoke. The horses were plodding along head-hung. Eventually, when Flaherty roused himself, they halted and dismounted to loosen cinches, drape bridles from saddlehorns, and let the animals graze for a while. The urgency that had driven them most of the day no longer seemed relevant. At least it did not appear to be, as Mike Flaherty sought a punky old deadfall log and sat on it, watching the far sky and its stubbornly lingering light.

Whit walked back through the trees. Carl Muller followed him. They stopped beside a little whitewater creek so narrow a man could step across it without straining, but a couple of feet deep. Whit dumped his hat, rolled under his neckband and knelt to wash his face, neck, and hair. Doctor Muller did the same a couple of yards distant. As they were mopping off as best they could, using bandannas and shirttails, Tom Hart walked up, sat on a punky stump, and said, "I'm hungry enough to eat the rear-end out of a snake if someone would hold its head, an' that old cowman said as soon as it's dark enough we're goin' to ride another few miles, then leave the horses, and go after those outlaws on foot, in the damned dark, in country I never been in before—with my belly thinkin' my throat's been cut."

Instead of commenting, Whit Pierson offered his lint-encrusted plug of molasses-cured. Tom recoiled as though the plug were a snake. Whit shrugged, pocketed the plug, and stood up, shaking water out of his hair.

Doctor Muller smoked cigars, but he had neglected to bring any with him, and because he did not even have that much to offer the harness maker he gave him some advice instead.

"Suffer in silence, Tom. You're no worse off than the rest of us. We'll find some grub directly."

Hart was not especially placated. "That's what old scrawny-bones said. I think he likes doing this. I don't think he's got a belly."

"Maybe not," Muller replied. "But he's got a heart."

They trooped back where the horses were slightly less distinct out where they were cropping grass. Doughbelly's bottle was leaning against a tree, empty. He and Flaherty had killed it, but it did not appear to have changed anything for either one of them. Flaherty sat, loosely relaxed, watching rusty-red clouds gradually losing color, and Doughbelly had scooped up a mound of soft pine needles, which he was sitting on. It was one of the unsolved mysteries of Dough-belly's life that anything stuffed with hay and grass could be as uncomfortably hard to sit on as a horse.

Flaherty looked around as Tom, Carl, and Whit emerged from the timber. "Might as well get to moving," he announced, and initiated the action by arising, brushing off his britches, and starting out where the horses were.

Later, when they were ready to mount, he fastened a steady look upon Carl and said, "I'd take it kindly if you'd answer a question for me, Doctor. What kind of a belly-gripe comes on gradual, gets worse for a few months, then takes a person off?"

Muller had his reins in his left hand and was leaning to mount as he replied. "I can't answer that, Mister Flaherty. Almost anything that happens down there acts like that, but mostly it don't kill people. I'm sorry." Muller grunted up into the saddle, eased down very gingerly, then said something else. "Keep the memory bright, Mister Flaherty."

As they were heading out again old Flaherty looked through the quickening gloom and nodded at Muller.

7

A Time of Darkness

THEY rode without haste. Flaherty was quiet, but his head was up. He rode facing ahead, and as Whit Pierson watched him it crossed Pierson's mind that the cowman was sorting out the country up ahead the way someone might do who was familiar with it.

Daylong springtime heat had soaked into trees, rocks, the ground itself. After sunset each of these things started giving off the stored heat, keeping things warm as the riders plodded ahead.

Old Flaherty swatted a mosquito on his stubbly cheek. Doughbelly, still riding stirrup with him, beat the air with his hat against the same annoying insects. Occasionally a horse would react to being bitten by vigorously wagging its tail.

As time passed and no moon appeared, Flaherty angled away from the trees; their backgrounding camouflage was no longer needed.

Creatures that hunted by night appeared: low-winging, rodent-hunting owls, some scuttling raccoons now and then, and a pair of foraging wolves who had no idea two-legged things were within a hundred miles of them until they ran out of the timber directly in the path of the oncoming horsemen. They halted for several seconds, dumbfounded, then fled with their belly guard hairs brushing the ground, each wolf taking a different course.

Flaherty watched them, right hand resting upon the upended butt plate of his saddle gun, no shred of empathy or admiration showing on his rugged face. When the big wolves had faded in the gloom, Flaherty removed his hand from the weapon and glanced at Doughbelly. "They're worse'n ticks. No matter how many a man shoots, next summer there'll be twice as many."

Doughbelly was dozing when his horse snorted, then shied violently, nearly losing its rider. The others reacted too, but not as fiercely. Flaherty held up a hand to stop everyone. While they were regaining their balance and control it was possible to hear very distinctly a large, heavy animal on their left somewhere, crashing through underbrush and small trees.

Tom Hart said, "Bear. Now what'n hell's she doing this time of night?"

No one answered. Flaherty continued northward another half mile, then stopped where the mosquitoes were particularly troublesome, swung to the ground, and waved his arms to ward off the insects as he said, "From here on, we walk an' lead the horses."

No one objected. They wouldn't have, in any case, because staying where they were was uncomfortable. But the mosquitoes followed them until they reached a place where young trees, and some that were not so young, were lying flat, all facing in the same direction. Flaherty slackened until he had passed the worst of the blow-downs, found something to tie his horse to, and pulled out his carbine. He grinned wolfishly at Doughbelly. "There are two lily ponds up ahead on the right, and about another mile upwards there's a lake where In'ian tipi rings pretty much surround the water. I figure those renegades are at the ponds or the lake. Most likely one of the ponds, because they'd come onto them before they'd find the lake."

Doctor Muller said, "That accounts for the mosquitoes."

Flaherty did not respond. He waited until all the horses had been tied, then said, "Carbines, gents. Stay behind me an' don't make any noise."

Whit was taking out his Winchester when Tom Hart said dryly, "That old devil can't be right all the time, can he?"

Whit grinned in the gloom. "You always get skeptical when your gut is empty. Come along."

"It's not just empty, partner. It's feedin' on itself."

Flaherty paused, grounded his weapon, and looked back. "Maybe we ought to set a spell until those two gents get their discussion finished." He turned and struck out again.

Doughbelly, who was directly behind the cowman, craned around a couple of times just before they passed from grass country into the trees. The others were walking in single file, with Tom Hart second from last.

There were fewer mosquitoes among the trees, but the few there were homed in on the warm human flesh. No one heeded them; walking in a crouch, old Flaherty was discernible in the lead, Winchesters held across his body in both hands.

He had not said how far the ponds were, only the distance to the lake, but it seemed to the men, trying not to make noise while simultaneously avoiding rough-barked big old trees in darkness, that they had walked at least a mile before the cowman stopped again, grounded his saddle gun, and leaned down on it.

The moon was just now inching over some jagged rims. Its light spread slowly across an area where the trees came no closer than about fifteen yards to a body of water that looked more like a farmed field. Lily pads were thick across its surface, the sound of frogs was loud and continuous, and except for the occasional places where lily pads had not monopolized the space and moonlight could reflect dully off still water, the impression was of some kind of farmed crop.

Flaherty leaned on a tree in silence. The others moved closer and either squatted or stood as they made slow sweeps of the entire treeless area, hoping to catch sight of a campfire.

Whit addressed the cowman, "Not here." Flaherty nodded

as he straightened up, hooked the carbine in the crook of one arm, and started eastward on a course that would lead them around the pond in a direction where the trees were not as thick, and where it was possible to see better.

Somewhere in the opposite direction a horse whinnied.

Everyone halted to look back. Charley Bonner spoke. "We're heading in the wrong direction."

Flaherty neither agreed nor disagreed, he simply walked past Bonner back the way they had come, and the others followed him.

Whit spoke in a half-whisper to the harness maker. "If we can set them afoot . . ."

Hart nodded without speaking. He was heading back again into dense timber where moonlight did not filter through. He could avoid most of the trees without much difficulty, but their roots were something else. He had almost tripped several times already. He preferred his manhunts in broad daylight.

Flaherty seemed to be able to see in the darkness. He sashayed around through the timber without slackening his pace. He stopped twice. The first time was when something fell from the high branches of a big tree as he was passing. He heard it coming and sprang ahead and to one side as though he had springs instead of boots on his feet.

It was a half-grown cinnamon bear, about the size of a young dog and so terrified it made no attempt to spring up and flee even after Doughbelly poked it with his carbine barrel. Flaherty shook his head at it, turned irritably, and stamped ahead, leaving the fate of the little creature to the men behind. They passed it, too. It did not move until they were out of sight, then it unrolled, stood up, and without even a backward glance went blindly running in the opposite direction, until it struck a tree head-on.

What ultimately alerted the manhunters that they were approaching a camp was the smell of wood smoke. Whit moved past Doughbelly and the stockman to make a soundless scout. Flaherty said nothing but watched the stage driver until he was lost to sight among the trees, then he squatted to wait. The others did the same. Doughbelly started to speak, but the old cattleman swung an arm to silence him.

A very faint sound of moving water came and went, sometimes very distinct, other times little more than a faint whisper. There was a bumbling little chilly wind blowing from west to east.

Whit wrinkled his nose at that as he slipped ahead. Something, anyway, was in their favor. If that whinnying horse was close and the wind had been blowing toward him and away from the possemen, instead of the other way around, the horse would have detected their scent and probably would have either fidgeted enough to be noticed or would have nickered again.

What Whit particularly watched for was firelight. The difficulty was that in a place as heavily timbered as this area was he might not be able to see it until he was very close.

But he did not see a light.

He moved impatiently, searching for it. The smoke smell was still discernible, so there had to have been a fire. It did not occur to him until he came to the edge of a lightning-strike meadow where no trees grew in an area of about twenty acres, that although the smoke scent was strong now, the fire itself did not have to be out in plain sight. On the north side of the glade, and on around it northwesterly, there was a thick jumble of huge rocks, black in color, with pockholes on them.

They were evidently what was left after a prehistoric eruption of some kind had hurled immense blocks of stone for miles, and that was where he finally saw a reflection of fitful pale light. It seemed to come from a cave or a similar variety of sheltered place in the rocks.

He sank to one knee, leaned on his Winchester, and looked for saddle animals somewhere out in the little glade. There were none, or if there were, they had to be across the grassy place being backgrounded by trees, because he could not see them.

He waited awhile, then started back. There would have to be a decision made about how the possemen and old Flaherty would challenge the men in that rocky place. They could spend the night moving soundlessly into position to command a view of the rocks and the glade, then face the outlaws when they came out in the morning for their animals, or they could creep up into the rocks and brace them there.

By the time he returned to his companions to report, Whit was of the opinion that the best course of action would be to infiltrate the little glade completely and wait for sunrise.

He explained everything to them, then whittled off a chew while they discussed the situation. On one point they all agreed; nothing could be done until morning. Doughbelly promptly curled up on a spongy bed of fragrant needles, pulled his hat down over his ears, and went to sleep.

Tom walked off and did not return for half an hour. Flaherty, Whit, Charley Bonner, and Doctor Muller squatted in stolid silence until Bonner mentioned Marshal Given. Then, the discussion livened up again. It was Bonner's opinion that they should surround the glade and throw down on the renegades when they came out in the morning for their saddlestock, because they'd probably leave Marshal Given behind, tied like a shoat, which would put him out of harm's way if a fight started.

Flaherty nodded at that. So did Carl Muller, but when Tom returned and they explained the plan to him, he said, "An' suppose these gents aren't that green? Suppose one of 'em stays in them rocks with Jack? Do we start a fight with the others? Because if we do, we're most likely goin' to get Jack shot."

Flaherty looked malevolently at the harness maker. "You got a better idea?"

Tom wasn't sure about that, but he had an idea. "Whit can guide us up where them boulders are. We can spend all night slitherin' in there an inch at a time if we got to. In the morning when they rise up but before they go after their horses we throw down on 'em, and if they even look like they might make trouble, or expect to use Jack Given as a shield, we just start firing."

From behind in the darkness a raspy voice said, "How do you know it's them outlaws? Hell, it could be pothunters or maybe prospectors. I'll tell you what I think—someone better scout that place out before sunrise to make sure we're after the right fellers, otherwise we'll have wasted all that damned time we've rode our butts sore gettin' up here."

Flaherty leaned to look over where Doughbelly was speaking from his curled position beside a huge old fir tree. He waggled his head. "He's dead right. If it's not them, an' they don't have your lawman prisoner, we'd ought to know now, not after sunup."

Whit turned away to spray amber and turned back without saying a word, but he was irritated. The odds against whoever was up in that glade not being the outlaws they were pursuing were, in his opinion, maybe a thousand to one. He became even more irritated when Bonner, Muller, and Flaherty looked steadily at him.

Tom Hart said, "I'll go with you," and got to his feet, leaned aside his carbine, and hitched his old holstered Colt into position.

Whit glared in Doughbelly's direction, but the saloonman was not looking. Whit did not say a word, simply got to his feet, put his saddle gun aside, jerked his head, and led the way back in the direction from which he had recently come.

When they were two thirds of the way to the glade and paused to test the night for sounds, Tom said, "You know why I volunteered to go with you?"

"Yeah. Because you figure whoever is up in those rocks's got something to eat."

The harness maker looked dumbfounded, but there was

no time to say anything because Whit was walking westerly again, slipping in and out among the trees.

When they reached the final fringe of forest and knelt, Whit raised his arm. "Watch up yonder. The fire was dyin' when I first saw it but . . . There! Did you see the light?"

Hart settled flat on the pine needles nodding his head. "Where are their horses?"

"Got to be over against the trees on the far side."

"You never saw them?"

"No."

"Whit, suppose instead of tryin' to sneak up yonder and get in among the rocks overlookin' their hideout, we go southward around this little glade, find their horses, catch them, and lead them away."

Pierson sat a long time in thought before speaking. "Yeah. The problem is, Tom, that when it comes down to them givin' up because they can't go anywhere without the horses, they got somethin' to trade us to get them back."

Hart slowly inclined his head. "Marshal Given." He unwound up off the ground, looking northward in the direction of all the volcanic rock. "Let's go," he said. "An' you was dead right—they better have grub in their camp, or I just might shoot them out of pure meanness."

8

End of a Long Night

THE smoke scent lingered, but those little fitful sparks of firelight no longer reflected off black rock as Whit and the harness maker picked their way northward where the uneven terrain tipped upward.

They eventually encountered some of the huge, pocked boulders that appeared to spread to the east and the west, where Whit had seen the firelight. What surprised them was that as they began working over and around the rocks, they discovered that the big rocks were not particularly heavy. At least not as heavy as other big rocks they had encountered elsewhere, and the smaller ones, not much larger than a man's head, were almost weightless.

In practical terms what this meant, and they both learned this quickly, was that while a huge boulder looked massive enough to be unaffected by two climbers scrambling over it, it was not massive at all. And unless they were careful, their combined weight made the boulders shift, grind against other stones, and in some cases, threaten to roll.

Whit was in the lead. He moved very slowly among the rocks, testing each one before putting any weight on it. They were losing time, but if they did not want to cause a noise that could be heard, they had no alternative. Tom's increasing impatience was approaching its zenith when Whit raised an arm and stopped on the north side of a deformed fir tree whose trunk curved around one of the big, pockmarked stones. Whit stood with his head cocked, listening.

Tom did not detect any sound, but he stood perfectly still, waiting to hear something.

Whit turned half around and pointed to their left with a stiff arm. Tom nodded, without any idea what Whit was doing but perfectly willing to follow, and tried to use Whit's boot marks as he moved westerly.

The night was silent—even nocturnal critters were avoiding noise but they were out there; they were always out there. A man could be quiet as a ghost, yet the forest inhabitants knew where he was and which way he was moving. Even when a man felt his safest, dozens of eyes watched him, dozens of ears heard him breathing.

Ordinary sounds that in daylight could go unnoticed, especially in a town, sounded twice as loud in the upland night. Up ahead of Whit and Tom someone coughed and expectorated. They froze in place until the silence returned, and Tom leaned to lightly tap Whit's shoulder. He said nothing, just gestured ahead and slightly southward in the direction of the noise. Whit nodded.

From this point onward the rocks were everywhere, some atop others, some in loose clutches with no room for walking between, and some seemingly teetering, awaiting the slightest blow to send them tumbling.

Whit was sweating before he had covered thirty yards in the new direction, and it was not a warm night; in fact, it had been getting steadily more chilly for the past couple of hours.

He used his hands more than his feet to test rocks they had to turn sideways to pass. He had to pause often because very little moonlight or starshine shone into this place, and small stones were underfoot.

The last time Whit halted to study a jumble of stones, Tom leaned and whispered to him, "We better go back for the others." Whit shook his head, still examining the rock pile up ahead.

Tom tapped him more insistently, and Whit finally turned to whisper. "We got this far. It can't be much farther. Maybe down below somewhere out near the glade beneath this big pile of stones. Beside, goin' back will take too long. It's going to be sunup directly. You go back if you want to."

Tom glared.

The best they could do as they approached the balancing boulders was pick a path either uphill above them or downhill toward the glade. Whit chose the downhill path. He knew what was down there but had no idea what might lie northward. For all he knew, it could be a miles-deep field of those big, unstable rocks.

A horse squealed in the distance. Whit stopped and Tom nearly bumped into him, muttering, "Damned mare."

Whit waited for someone to move, curse, or maybe cough again. Nothing happened, so he began inching onward, but now he was seeking places to put his feet that were downhill; for whatever reason, going downhill was easier. There were still unstable rocks on both sides, but there were also crooked pathways that were traversible. Occasionally their passage was blocked by a large stone. Whit would motion for Tom to retrace his steps, but this did not happen often.

They had no idea how much time they had used up, nor did they particularly think about it. Whit had had no illusions after his first view of the lava-rock field. He had told the others at the palaver what they would probably encounter, but he'd had no idea how extensive or treacherous the rock field would be.

A horse squealed again and this time another horse snorted back loudly. Again they had to stop and wait. This time, though, a sleep-thickened growly voice said, "I told you not to take that mare, Fred. I told you she was horsing."

A sharper voice replied. "You told me a lot of things Curt, an' look where it's got us. At least, the mare had saddle marks. That horse you roped for me was unbroke sure as hell."

Curt said, "It's time to roll out anyway . . . We might have to cross open country goin' back. It'd be better to do that before daylight. How's the prisoner doing?"

"See for yourself," Fred replied irritably. "Them damned horses will be a mile off an' I'm not much on walking."

For a moment there was silence, then Curt said, "Keep an eye open out there. Fred?"

"What?"

"Stay to the trees. Sure as hell they're behind us somewhere."

Fred was not in a good mood. "They're always behind us. They was behind us up in Montana. They're behind us down here. We should have listened to that friend of yours at the bank up north and stopped the damned coach out in the middle of nowhere an' taken the boxes off, but no, you was greedy an' wanted to raid the bank where they delivered them boxes and get more. And what did we get? A ride out of Beaverton, a pouch with only two thousand dollars in it— and they're behind us again."

Curt was briefly silent, then he said, "We'll lose them. Since we been ridin' I been losin' posses time after time, ain't I? And this time we'll give them somethin' to remember as long as they live."

Fred was moving when he replied. Whit and Tom could hear his boots rattling gravel when he said, "It might have worked before, Curt. It's too damned dangerous now, an' we don't even know if that damned bank has any more money in it."

"It's got money in it," a different voice said, a higher, more youthful voice. "You seen that town, Fred. Prosperous as all hell. They got lots of money in that bank. Curt's right."

Fred snarled a fierce epithet and rattled more gravel as he walked away.

Tom leaned against a rock and gazed at Whit. In a whisper he said, "You know what they're figurin' to do, for crissake— go back to Beaverton and rob the bank. I don't believe it. They're crazy."

Whit was feeling around for his plug, and he did not reply until he had a small cud snugged into his cheek, then all he whispered was, "How fast can we get the hell back down out of here?"

Tom started to turn back when a man's angry profanity halted him. It was the man with the youthfully high voice. Then the man said, "I'm goin' to shoot him, Curt. I told you yesterday, draggin' him along was a waste of time. We should have left him under the coach with the other one."

His deep, growly voice sounded rougher as Curt replied, "Put up that gun. You're not goin' to do any such thing. You put up that gun or I'll blow your buckle past your backbone. . . . Now then, he didn't chew all the way through the rope, did he?"

"No, but he would have in another little while. Curt, he's a nuisance. We can't afford to herd him along, not with them other ones somewhere behind us."

"We take him along. I'll tell you why—because he's known in that town. He lives there, an' he's goin' to take us into that bank like we was friends of his. Maybe afterward, when we're ready to leave, we'll shoot him, but not now. Gather some twigs and get the fire goin', will you?"

Whit ranged a glance toward the northern skyline, the only direction treetops did not hinder his view. The sky had a streaked, fishbelly color to it. False dawn. Daylight was still a while off.

Tom wagged his head and rolled his eyes. He offered to say nothing, which was just as well because Whit gestured for him to move along, back the way they had come.

Whit urged Tom to make better time as they withdrew toward the forest, exactly as Tom had tried to urge Whit to pick up the gait a little when they'd been making their way into the jumble of rocks, and Tom took this urging about as well as Whit had. He scowled.

Daylight arrived by the time they were back down where they had first entered the rock field. Tom might have stopped, but Whit walked past him without looking around or saying a word. He was taking long steps.

Tom protested, but mildly, because he knew why Whit was hastening. Whit looked over his shoulder briefly and grinned. "Food isn't everything, you old goat. If you wasn't so skinny an' had stored up fat like normal folks, you wouldn't be hungry."

"Is that so? I suppose you aren't hungry?"

Whit continued to make haste in the direction of the place where their companions would be waiting. He did not reply, so the harness maker said no more.

Whit halted abruptly, facing west. Out through the trees where new daylight had brightened the glade, a lean, leggy man was riding one horse bareback with a squaw-bridle and herding other horses in the direction of the lava-rock camp of his companions.

Tom moved among the trees to get closer. Whit went after him and rapped him on the back. "Stand still."

"I could blow him off that horse from here."

"You probably could. Then where would we be? The other two would hightail up into the mountains and we'd lose them sure as hell."

Tom groaned aloud. "You see what he's doing?"

"Yeah. Chewin' on a piece of jerky. Come along."

Hart turned back, but as they were moving away he said, "I could break his neck for that jerky."

Whit continued to whip in and out among the trees until he smelled horses, then slackened off a little, looking for Flaherty and the men who had ridden from town with him.

What he saw was a tethered horse partially saddled, but there were no men until both he and Tom got closer, then they appeared with Winchesters. Tom looked at them disgustedly. "Who'd you figure we was, Jesse James an' the Youngers?"

Old Flaherty glared, but grounded his weapon long enough to finish saddling. He said, "Took you long enough.

We was about to ride up through there and smoke 'em out without you."

All talk and movement stopped when Whit and Tom related what they had heard. When silence returned, Charley Bonner, Walt Coggins, Doughbelly, and even the old cowman were staring at them.

It was Charley who finally spoke. "Rob my bank? Go all the way back to town and rob my bank? That's the craziest thing I ever heard."

Doctor Muller was chewing a little ball of pitch, which he spat out before speaking. "Crazy or not, we better get down out of here and head for home. If we don't get there before they do . . ." He did not finish as he went over to complete rigging out his horse.

It was the old cowman who accepted most readily the idea of the outlaws who had robbed the stage, killed the guard, and stolen his horses, planning to rob the bank in Beaverton. He slammed a Winchester into its scabbard, cheeked his horse to mount as it turned toward him, and spoke to the others from the saddle.

"It's always a horse race, boys. I never yet taken up the trail after renegades when it hasn't been a horse race. Mostly, it goes on a long while with me tryin' to keep them in sight, an' them tryin' not to let me do that." He watched them get astride and raised his rein-hand to lead off back down through the timber as he completed his statement. "This time it won't be no different, unless you want to go back to the meadow and see if we can smoke those gents out, an' hang 'em up in here if we're successful. And maybe bury your lawman in the process."

Charley Bonner did not even look at Mike Flaherty as he urged his horse crossways down the slope. He had only one thing in his mind; neither hunger, thirst, weariness, nor a rubbed-raw behind could intrude against that one thing. As he started past old Flaherty he said, "Not my bank. By gawd, not my bank, if I got to ride this horse to death to get back to town."

Flaherty peered from beneath his hatbrim and pensively scratched the top of his nose as he moved in behind the banker. "You ride that horse to death, mister, and when he goes down you will too, with a bullet through your lights. Now hold up an' let me take the lead. You're not heading right anyway. I said hold up!"

Flaherty got the lead, the others were strung out behind him. Somewhere far back Doughbelly called out, "Hey! Why give 'em a chance to reach town? Why not set up an ambush right here among these trees, and as they ride past, blow 'em out'n their saddles?"

Charley turned fiercely on Doughbelly. "And suppose they get away, or suppose something else goes wrong? We're not going to take any chances, Doughbelly. We're not going to do a damned thing that'll endanger our chance of reaching town ahead of them." Charley paused. "There's eight thousand dollars in the vault."

Muller and Coggins exchanged a look. So did Hart and Pierson. The banker had reason to be worried about his bank. It was old Flaherty who settled things by saying, "They most likely could be bushwhacked up in here—unless instead of coming back down this way they go on up over the rims an' down the other side toward Beaverton, which is what I'd do in their boots. And we'd be settin' here all day twiddlin' our thumbs."

"Mister Bonner's right. We got to beat them to Beaverton . . ."

9

Aiming for Beaverton

DOUGHBELLY did not look as though he was convinced this plan of more saddle-backing was better than his suggestion of an ambush, but he followed along without another word until they were beginning to feel daylight-heat down where the forest thinned out and they could see open country to the west.

Old Flaherty did not leave the timber until he had to, staying among the trees not for shade but to mask their movement in the event anyone back up yonder might be watching.

Whit admired the old man. He told Tom that if anyone had ever out-Indianed the Indians, it was Mike Flaherty. Hart was in his disputatious mood again. "An' the army," he said sourly as they left the trees by way of a long spit that pointed like an arrowhead in the direction of the distant stage road.

Doctor Muller was up beside the old cowman when he said he was too old for this kind of damned foolishness, and was speared by a searing stare as Flaherty replied to that.

"Not too old, Doctor, too punky soft. Age is a number, like countin' cattle through a gate. You're old when you let your carcass run down on you."

Muller turned, put a hopeless look upon Walt Coggins, and allowed Flaherty to get ahead before he said, "There is something else you do when you age, Walt. He's a prime example. You get ideas fixed in your mind until there's no longer room for flexibility. Then you butt your head against everything you can't tolerate."

The storekeeper was watching Flaherty. "How old would you say he is?"

Muller's brow furrowed, his lips pursed. "It's hard to say. Maybe seventy-five. Maybe eighty."

Coggins commented dryly. "I think I'll cultivate some of those pigheaded notions. He sets a horse like he was twenty, and he don't seem to get tired."

Charley Bonner pushed up ahead to ride with the old cowman. He'd paid no attention to the discussions, he had just one thing on his mind. When Flaherty lifted his horse into a lope on a diagonal course toward the distant stage road, Charley loped beside him, unmindful of his tender cheeks. When Flaherty showed a wolfish grin, Charley said, "What are our chances?"

Flaherty continued to grin wickedly. "They got to go over the rims an' down the other side. That's hard on horseflesh. They maybe can cut the distance in half, Mister Banker, but we can travel faster because we're goin' over level country. Remember what I said? It'll be a horse race. But not for speed so much as for endurance. If they push their animals, they're not goin' to be able to keep it up. We're not goin' to ride that hard."

The banker's worried look increased. "It'll still be neck-and-neck? Is that what you're saying?"

Flaherty didn't reply; someone was loping up on his left side. He twisted to see who it was. When he recognized Whit Pierson he hauled down to a steady walk. "Nice day," he said, and smiled disarmingly.

Whit ignored the statement and the smile as he raised his right arm to point dead ahead where the distant roadbed was visible as a straight north-south pencil-thin line that reflected sunlight. "Straighten out an' head directly for the roadway," he said.

Flaherty's smile faded as he kept his unwavering gaze on the younger man. "You got a reason?" he asked.

"Yeah. We've used these animals pretty hard, Mister Flaherty."

"Yes, we have, for a fact, but they're fresher'n the ones those renegades are riding."

Whit squinted at the direction of the sun before speaking again. "The road is maybe two miles east." He brought his head down and looked at the older man. "The Livermore northbound stage should be showin' up to the south within the next hour or maybe less. It'll have fresh animals on the pole."

Flaherty's gaze did not waver, but it narrowed slightly. He barely inclined his head as he spoke. "You're a stage driver, eh? An' you've maybe made that run, have you?"

"I'd guess about three, four hundred times over the past ten years."

Flaherty twisted to look back at the others, then sat forward, lifted his left hand, and squeezed his horse. When he broke over into a lope on an altered, due-east course, the others did the same. He did not look at Whit again until they could make out details of the roadway, then he pulled down to a walk and said, "Where is it?"

Whit was not disconcerted by the absence of a stagecoach even after he stood in his stirrups looking southward for sign of it. He sat down as he answered. "It will be along."

Flaherty accepted that. So did everyone else, but as they walked their horses the last mile or so, each one of them watched the southward country until Doughbelly, no longer bringing up the drag, gestured and called out. "Yonder. Hard to see because the gap's directly behind him, but look a little higher. See the dust?"

They saw it and watched it. The stage was not approaching fast. Flaherty looked back at Doughbelly and said, "Come up here. You got good eyes, saloonman."

Doughbelly sat erect in the saddle. He had every right to.

People like old Flaherty were almighty sparing with compliments. Doughbelly forgot his sore bottom as he urged the horse ahead.

Whit left them without a word, loped almost up to the berm of the roadway, and sat his horse, watching the oncoming dust. By the time the others came up it was possible to discern that the oncoming vehicle was indeed a stagecoach.

Doctor Muller watched it, too, but with a worried look. "If we string out across the road to stop it," he opined, "and there's a guard along, he's going to think we're highwaymen."

The banker's worried look was on the stagecoach when Whit replied. "Yeah. You fellers stay here. I'll ride down to it. I don't know which driver is up there, but he'll know who I am."

Tom said, "I hope so," as Whit rode parallel to the road directly toward the stagecoach. While he rode he fished around for his handkerchief, which was a large red bandanna, tied it to the tip of his saddlegun, and kept it in his lap until he was sure the whip and guard could see it, then he held the carbine above his head and waved it back and forth.

The coach did not slacken off, but it had not been moving fast anyway. Whit could see the gun-guard, who was a darkly bearded man, lean to say something to the whip while at the same time raising a long-barreled rifle from between his knees to his lap.

Whit continued to signal with the red bandanna and the stage continued to approach at a slogging walk. He recognized the driver but not the gun-guard. He lowered the Winchester to his lap, cupped both hands, and yelled.

"Hubbard! Henry Hubbard."

They heard him. Hubbard and the gun-guard conversed briefly, then the whip hauled back to stop his outfit and the guard went swiftly down to the ground, stepped very close to the coach on the near side, rested his rifle atop a steel tire, and called ahead. "What do you want? Who are you?"

Instead of replying, Whit dropped his carbine, tossed his six-gun after it, held both hands shoulder high, and kneed the horse forward until the driver suddenly called out, sounding startled. "Buffler, don't shoot. That's Whit Pierson."

The guard did not raise his head from low down above the rifle's sights when he said, "Who is Whit Pierson?"

"He's one of Holt's drivers. Drove for us longer'n anyone else . . . Hey, Whit, what's wrong? Who is that up yonder?"

"Doctor Muller, Walt Coggins, Charley Bonner, and Doughbelly. Henry, tell that guard to point his rifle some other way."

The driver gave an order; Buffler straightened up, grounded his weapon, and waited until Whit was prepared to halt near the head of the leaders when he said, "You named four of 'em, Mister Pierson, an' there's five riders settin' up there."

"The fifth one is a rancher named Flaherty from over against the mountains." Having answered the wary gun-guard Whit raised his face to the man on the high seat. "Henry, you got passengers?"

"No. Light freight for the general store."

"Henry, it's a long story but we're after the outlaws who are holding the marshal prisoner, shot Dan Crockett, and dumped the coach down into a gully, and we're racin' against time. We need to ride in your coach up to Beaverton."

Buffler set his rifle in the crook of one arm and moved forward until he was looking up at Whit. "We heard some of this. Beaverton's buzzin' with it. When Mister Holt come back with Crockett's body and the banged-up coach there was a lot of fuss." Buffler leaned to look up where the waiting horsemen sat, then turned and spoke to the driver. "Henry, you're the boss."

The driver did not even hesitate. "Signal 'em to come on

down here, Whit. What are you goin' to do with your horses?"

"Turn 'em loose. We'll dump our outfits in the boot." He waved his hat and as his companions started toward the coach Tom Hart swung off, retrieved Pierson's weapons, remounted, and rode ahead, shaking his head about dropping weapons in dirt.

Flaherty was the first to free his animal. He led it out a short distance, pointed it toward the distant mountains, slapped it on the rump, and shrugged as he watched it lope free. Sometimes they went home and sometimes they didn't.

As he was walking back, the others followed his example after pitching their saddles, blankets, and bridles into the boot.

Whit was feeling around for the smidgin that remained of his cut plug when the bearded guard came over and pushed out a hand not much smaller than a ham. "Buffler Stoneman. I wouldn't have pointed the gun, except that I didn't know—"

"It's all right," Whit said, pumped the hand, and resumed his search until he found the little scrap and began picking lint off it as Buffler spoke again. "I'm new. Got hired on with Mister Holt to replace Dan Crockett. Ain't been in the country long." Stoneman eyed the shred of cut plug. "If you want a chaw between here'n town, just rap on the roof. I got plenty."

Whit was the last one inside the coach. They'd had to unload several crates to make room for everyone, and even then, it was crowded. Henry Hubbard had been hesitant about abandoning the crates until the man whose store they were destined for helped offload them.

Buffler Stoneman went up the side of the rig to his perch, leaned the rifle aside, and braced as Hubbard kicked the binders off and whistled up his hitch. There was a jolt, then the rig settled down to its customary pitching, swaying motion. Tom Hart found the remnants of someone's travel mixture and after offering it around, and watching hawklike as the others helped themselves, settled beside the door, eating what remained.

For a mile nothing was said, but as the men relaxed, Carl Muller made an observation that he had made many times before. "If Sam would replace these damned leather thoroughbrace springs with the new steel ones, it wouldn't make people seasick every time they had to ride one of his stages."

For once Tom Hart did not take an opposing stand. He was finishing the last crumbs from the little oily brown paper sack he had found.

They were cramped shoulder to shoulder, particularly where the doctor and storekeeper sat. They were both thick-bodied men. At least, Tom Hart and Mike Flaherty were lean.

Doughbelly snored. Doctor Muller eyed him with a mixture of envy and disgust. Anyone who could sleep on a stagecoach, even one with newfangled leaf-steel springs, had to be more animal than human.

Whit gazed at his companions. Every one of them looked like something a pup would drag out of a tanyard: unshaven, sunken-eyed, dirty, bedraggled. Old Flaherty caught his eye and slowly winked.

Doughbelly's snoring was interrupted when the stage struck a chuckhole. The wheels dropped into it with a jolt and were hauled up out of it with another jolt. Tom looked at his friend. "He's doin' real good, isn't he? Hasn't missed a single pothole since we got aboard."

Whit's response was about as Tom's normally was. He took the opposite stand. "He's young, Tom. It takes time to learn how to avoid the deep ones." Having had his say, Whit leaned and sprayed tobacco juice out the off-side window.

Doughbelly's snoring started up again, and Carl Muller looked in the opposite direction as he said, "They might not get to town until after nightfall."

That idea did not find much support, mainly because no one wanted to have to engage the outlaws when it was too dark to see well. The first to dispute the doctor was, naturally, the harness maker. He scoffed. "They can get up there before sundown. Once they get over the rims an' down the north slope they got open country all the way."

Flaherty said, "On wore-down horses."

The banker liked Muller's notion. "It'll be easier to fort up inside the bank in the dark. If they wait until nightfall, they'll never get inside. I'll see to that."

Someone's sharp elbow brought Doughbelly awake. He listened to the conversation for a while, straightened up, moved his shoulders to get a little clearance, then leaned to look out, not at the countryside particularly, but at the shadows, at their depth and angles of slant. By his estimate it was mid-afternoon. He settled back, shouldering for more room again, as he spoke. "What was that you'n Tom said last night, Whit? They figured to use Marshal Given to get them inside the bank? Well, they must not be planning on getting in when the bank is closed. Every town I ever been in, the bank closed about sundown. If they still figure to do that, gents, they won't try it until tomorrow."

Doughbelly crossed his arms, composed himself as best he could for rest, and with the others looking at him, closed his eyes.

10

Back Home

THEIR arrival in Beaverton went almost completely unnoticed, but that did not last long. It was a little early for the widowers and bachelors to be drifting over to the café, but there were several diners at the counter when all five possemen walked in and began ordering even before they were seated. Soon news of their arrival was broadcast by other diners, as well as by the same dayman who had outfitted them when they'd left. But unlike the caféman, who was a jovial individual and greeted everyone heartily, the livery barn hostler saw them entering the café and rushed up there to ask about the horses he had rented them. Tom Hart answered while the others went after the cups of hot java that had been set before them. Tom had his fingers around the cup when he looked around at the hostler.

"We left 'em at a foothill ranch quite a distance from here. They're in good hands. Someone will go fetch them for you directly, but right now we got more important things to worry about."

"You turned them loose over against them mountains?" the dayman asked, dumbfounded.

"No. We left 'em at a ranch owned by a gent named Flaherty. They'll be fine until—"

"Flaherty? Not a feller named Mike Flaherty? My boss says he's meaner'n a boar bear an' never gives strays back if they're on his land when he catches 'em."

Tom raised his cup and soberly regarded it as the others

turned slowly to regard the agitated hostler. Whit Pierson said dryly, "Partner, you can tell your boss we'll bring back his horses as soon as we can, an' you can tell him you just met a friend of ours—this here is Mike Flaherty."

The hostler looked like he would faint. Old Flaherty did not offer his hand; he sat there staring malevolently until the hostler fled, and as the door closed behind him, Flaherty slapped Whit on the shoulder and everyone laughed, including the caféman.

They were scarfing up food without a sound except for the rattle of eating utensils when Sam Holt walked in accompanied by the gun-guard Buffler Stoneman. Buffler grinned, but Sam didn't. He peered through his thick glasses and said, "Is it true they're comin' this way?" He did not say who might be coming and he did not have to, but for a time no one answered because to do so would interrupt their eating. Doctor Muller finally replied, right after swallowing one mouthful and before taking another one.

"Seems like they are. To raid the bank. Maybe tonight, but more likely tomorrow."

Muller went back to his meal, but Charley Bonner, whose appetite had been less ravenous because of anxiety, arose, spilled silver coins atop the counter, and stepped away to take Sam's arm and lead him outside.

The next diner to leave was Doughbelly, and he took Mike Flaherty with him, not entirely because of the friendship that had developed between them over the past couple of days but because Doughbelly owned the Beaverton Waterhole Saloon.

Walt Coggins eventually paid for his meal and also departed. He went first to the store to fill a pocket with stogies, then headed for his residence, where Mrs. Coggins had been on pins and needles since he'd left and could be expected to make sure Walt understood what his riding with the town possemen had put her through; a man his age, with his responsibilities and all, riding out of town with his coattail flapping, like he was some twenty-year-old flibbertigibbet!

Doctor Muller left the harness maker and Whit Pierson in front of the café as he headed for his cottage to bathe, change clothing, shave, and stand—not sit—out back where he raised a few flowers, with a waterglass of Scotch whiskey for companionship. Where nothing moved or talked or itched or smelled like a horse.

Whit went over to the harness works with Tom, who made the mistake of not locking his roadside door. He set up a bottle and two greasy little jolt glasses on the counter, poured them full from behind the counter, and pushed one toward Whit, who was on the customer side of the counter. Tom removed his shellbelt and weapon, draped them from a wall peg, tossed his hat aside, reached inside his shirt, and vigorously scratched. "Eight thousand dollars for crissake? He told me one time he didn't keep more'n maybe a thousand in cash on hand."

Whit was toying with his glass. "You remember one of them saying something about a bank clerk up north telling them they ought to stop my stage and rob it before it got down this far?"

Tom nodded while dropping his whiskey straight down. "Yeah. I thought about that on the stage. Seems likely the only way we're goin' to find out what he meant is after we catch 'em."

"What he meant," stated Whit, "is that someone up north, probably where they loaded that money, or at some bank up there where they stored it until it was loaded, was in cahoots with them."

"Must be quite a friend. The best a friend ever done for me was talk me into joinin' the town posse," Tom said, and kept his eyes on the bottle as he refilled their glasses.

Whit waited for the taller man's eyes to lift, then he replied. "I didn't talk you into anything. You're too pigheaded to be talked into something. I just said we needed another man or two, and you volunteered." Whit raised his glass, still looking straight at his old friend. "Here's to old Flaherty."

Tom raised his glass. "For a damned fact. I still don't much care for the old bastard, but we'd sure never have got much done without him."

This time they put the glasses and bottle aside. Tom fed kindling into his little iron stove, fired the thing, and set the damper before returning to the far side of his counter to hoist a lamp mantle, light an untrimmed wick, lower the mantle, and make an adjustment so that late-day shadows would be kept at bay. When he turned back he was scowling. "Jack's between a high fence an' a kickin' mule. If he makes it, he'll have a story to tell."

"He'll make it, Tom."

"Yeah, Of course he will . . . but in case he don't it'd only be right for someone to track those men down an' leave 'em hangin' in a tree somewhere."

The local blacksmith and two other men walked in. Tom swiftly put his bottle on a shelf beneath the counter, ignored the little glasses, and said, "Evening, gents. The shop is closed for doin' business."

The blacksmith was a short man built like an oak barrel, scarred, massive, and slate-eyed. He was lined and graying, with a testy disposition, which went with his trade; it was hard to wake up every morning wearing a smile and full of fondness for humanity when the day before you'd been kicked by some damned horse whose owner had deliberately lied to you by saying his animal was dog-gentle because he knew if he told the truth you wouldn't shoe him.

The blacksmith nodded. "It's goin' around town that the band of outlaws that got away from you boys is headin' this way to rob the town and shoot up the place. Fifteen of 'em—leftovers from some wartime guerilla band. What we'd like to know is—where is Jack Given?"

Neither Whit nor Tom spoke for a long time. They leaned

on the counter, gazing at the blacksmith and his two companions.

Whit finally spoke. "There are three of them, Wes, not no fifteen. We got no idea who they are or what they did before they killed Crockett and stole the pouch of money. And they got Jack with them. They figure to use him to get into town and raid the bank. They figure to do that because they don't expect we know anything about their plan, or that they are comin' back here. They didn't get away from us. Tom an' I got into some rocks and listened to them talking. That's how we know what they're goin' to try to do. And one more thing, Wes. They never saw any of us an' we never saw any of them. They got no idea we heard them and hightailed it back to town to be here when they ride in."

One of the blacksmith's companions, a tall, lean man with an Adam's apple that bobbled when he talked, had a question: "You're plumb certain Given isn't ridin' with them?"

Both Pierson and Hart stared at the man, then Hart began to get red in the face. "Is that what's goin' around town? Who the hell are you, anyway?"

"My name is Fadiman. I'm the new clerk at Leathergood's abstract office."

Tom dropped his gaze to the blacksmith. "You sure gone down in the world when you'll run with something like that one, Wes."

The blacksmith fidgeted, shot a fierce look at the tall man, and without another word stamped back out to the roadway. Whit and Tom watched him light into the tall man as though he might eat him alive.

"People," the harness maker said with a scornful snort. He felt around beneath the counter for the bottle he'd cached. "You ever feel you liked the horses you drove better'n some of the people you knew, Whit?"

"Lots of times, Tom. In fact maybe most of the time . . . No thanks. No more or I won't be able to find my rear end with both hands. I'm goin' home to clean up." As Whit faced the door he also said, "I'll be back directly. We better all get together again, either over at Doughbelly's place or in here, and figure out what we got to do. For one sure fact, folks got to be warned to stay away from Main Street tonight an' tomorrow. Another thing, we got to have some men patrol town tonight."

Tom nodded. "And first thing in the morning, before sunup, put some fellers over west of town with steel mirrors."

But Whit did not return directly. He made the mistake of brewing a pot of coffee and taking a cup of it to a chair where he could sit down, cock his feet on a little bench, and relax with his java.

He finished the coffee, which was all he remembered until someone pounding on his door brought him awake with a galloping heart. The caller was Sam Holt, peering like an owl from behind his thick glasses. As Whit moved aside for Holt to enter, the stage-company owner said, "Everybody's up at Doughbelly's place. Tom said you'd be along."

Whit yawned behind an upraised hand, scratched his head, and considered his former employer, who looked agitated, but since it had never taken much to upset Sam Holt, Whit was unmoved. He said, "Care for a cup of coffee?"

Holt's magnified eyes shone behind lenses that reflected lamplight. "No thanks. We shouldn't keep 'em waiting, Whit." He hesitated, cleared his throat, let his eyes jump away and back, then said, "I really didn't think you was in any danger, bringin' that money down here on your coach, I guess that was kind of simpleminded of me. As things turned out— hell—you brought those outlaws right into town with you. Like in a book I read one time about some fellers who made a big wooden horse, climbed into the thing, and when someone pulled their horse into town, they jumped out and shot up the place."

Whit went over to look into his empty cup. He refilled it with his back to Sam Holt. "Sure you don't want some, Sam?"

"Well . . . yeah, I'd like a cup. Whit?"

"No. Right now I don't even want to think about drivin' for you again, Sam."

They faced each other, cups in hand. Holt made little ripples in his cup without making an effort to raise the cup to his mouth. "Dan Crockett's widow is in a hell of a fix. Seems he drank up his pay before he ever got home with it. Most of it anyway." Sam finally tasted the coffee. "I sent her a hunnert dollars yesterday right after we buried Dan."

Whit emptied his cup, looked for his hat and coat, shifted the shellbelt, which had worked around until his holstered Colt was directly in front, and went to hold the door for Sam to precede him.

It was dark but there was a moon; a larger one than there had been the previous few nights, and it was also getting chilly. Whit asked what time it was. Sam pulled out his watch, flipped open the face, and held it up to within six inches of his face, then made a nervous little self-conscious smile and shoved it toward his companion. "I can't quite make it out in the dark."

Whit looked down. "Hell, I must have slept five or six hours. It's damned near midnight."

"You needed it," replied the stage-company owner, pocketing his watch. "From what I heard at the saloon, you fellers didn't eat or sleep for a hell of a long while."

"Too long," stated Whit. He looked at his companion. "Have you heard the gossip that Jack is riding with the outlaws?"

Evidently Holt had heard this, but he did not admit it. He simply said, "You can hear anything in this town. All you got to do is wait for someone who don't like you to think of a reason to make up lies, and before you know it, the lies are all over town. Jack Given's their prisoner. Tom told us that. So did the other possemen." Holt looked slightly bemused. "Doughbelly's got his badge. That's most likely what kept him alive. If those outlaws knew he was a lawman . . . Hell, they killed Dan Crockett when they didn't even know he couldn't hit the broad side of a barn from the inside, with a carbine or a rifle."

They were stopped midway along by a vigilant younger man who stepped out of a dog-trot with a Winchester in both hands. Holt was startled, but Whit shook his head at the man. "You had ought to let folks pass you, make sure you know them, then, if you don't know them, throw down on them from behind. You won't get shot so quick that way."

The vigilante was embarrassed. He muttered an apology and slunk back into his hiding place between two buildings.

Evidently while Whit had been sleeping someone had taken it upon himself to organize a party of vigilantes to mind the town, which Whit thought was an excellent idea even though he had long ago adopted Doughbelly's notion that if the renegades came at all, they would do so in daylight.

Sam Holt concealed his nervous recovery from facing a gunbarrel by removing his glasses and polishing them as they approached the saloon, which was brilliantly lighted. Whit watched this operation with wry interest. Polishing a pair of glasses while walking up a dark plankwalk was funny, especially in Sam's case because he couldn't see very well with clean glasses in broad daylight.

11

Flaherty Was Right

DOUGHBELLY was in hog-heaven: his saloon held about half the male residents of Beaverton, all were buying drinks, the air was splendidly fragrant from cigars and pipes, though less fragrant where cigarette smokers were congregating. Everyone seemed to be talking at the same time. Doughbelly had fired up his cast-iron cannon heater. When Whit entered, trailed by Sam Holt, heat hit them like a forge fire, along with the aroma and the noise.

Tom Hart and Mike Flaherty had taken their bottle and glasses to a corner table. Both were smoking cigars, sitting relaxed, watching the commotion. Tom raised an arm to flag Whit over, and when the stage driver sat down, old Flaherty pushed the bottle and his little sticky glass forward as he spoke loudly enough to be heard. "I was tellin' Tom it's been ten years since I been in such a noisy saloon. Doughbelly's makin' money faster'n he can shovel it in."

Whit poured his liquor glass full and nodded at Tom. The harness maker's ruddy complexion was a little redder than usual and sweat shiny. He winked at Whit, then spoke. "You missed the best part. Couple of fights darn near broke out when they was organizin' things. The blacksmith was linin' up vigilantes to patrol town tonight, with other gents to take over about sunrise, an' Charley Bonner wanted five of 'em hid inside the bank. Wes figured Charley was tryin' to take over and got mad."

Whit downed the whiskey, then nodded his head and

looked around the room until he saw the slate-eyed blacksmith, who also looked slightly red in the face and sweaty.
Even when he hadn't been drinking, the blacksmith was an
easily aroused individual.

Tom laughed. "For a spell it looked like everyone was goin'
to take one side or the other."

Whit raised his eyebrows and Mike Flaherty, who was
sitting sprawled, hat tipped far forward, finished the story.
"Doughbelly fired off a round, an' after that when you could
hear a pin drop he lit into both of 'em. That ended it."

"Who got his way?" Whit asked.

"Both of 'em. But Charley's got to pay a silver dollar to the
fellers who stay in the bank tonight an' tomorrow. The
blacksmith kept charge of the others."

Whit pushed the little glass toward Flaherty. It had been
his glass to start with. He put an inquisitive look upon the
harness maker. "What's been settled?" he asked.

"Just about everthing. There's watchers through town tonight with Winchesters. In the morning some other gents
spell them off. A few fellers been assigned to keepin' folks
away from Main Street tomorrow. That feller with the whiskers who was the gun-guard on Hubbard's stage yesterday,
him and two other men volunteered to scout out westerly
before sunup with mirrors. An' that's about it, except that
everyone in town is sittin' on pins an' needles. Sam's scairt
pea-green about sendin' out his stages tomorrow, an' Walt
Coggins is goin' to put up his steel window shields."

Flaherty looked faintly amused at the scene in front of
him. The last time he had been involved in anything like this
had been about twenty years back down at Livermore when
someone had said an Indian war party was on the way to
burn the town. It hadn't happened, because no war party
appeared; they never did discover who started the rumor.

Flaherty jutted his jaw toward the noisy confusion and
said, "Puts me in mind of a corralful of horsing mares. An'
the way they got things planned no outlaw with an eye in his

head isn't goin' to notice the empty roadway, the fellers skulkin' around carryin' Winchesters, and the shuttered store windows. Mister Stage Driver, we rode our butts off to get over here and lay a trap. There's not goin' to be any trap, just an armed town waitin' to kill outlaws, an' if the outlaws been at their trade any length of time, they'll smell this before they get into town."

Tom took his customary opposing position. "They'll try it, Mister Flaherty, because they don't have a lick of sense among the three of them. If they did have, they wouldn't come within a hundred miles of Beaverton for the rest of their lives. Not after what they done around here." Tom downed another jolt, blinked furiously for a moment, then wagged his head at the old cowman. "Because they don't have a lick of sense, they'll try it."

Flaherty looked straight ahead throughout the harness maker's statement and continued to do so afterward without saying a word. But Whit had the feeling that the cowman had not been influenced at all by what Tom Hart had said.

Charley Bonner approached the table, dragged up a chair, and raised a sleeve to wipe off sweat before he said, "That old man who runs the abstract office said a town full of grown men ought to be ashamed of themselves. Twenty, thirty of us acting like an army's comin' against us instead of just three measly outlaws."

Flaherty's eyes twinkled ironically as though these were also his exact thoughts, but all he said was, "You got men inside your bank, Mister Bonner?"

"Yes. Four of them and I'd have had more if it hadn't been for the blacksmith."

Flaherty continued to looked amused. "That's more'n there are outlaws. Do you know those boys real well, Mister Bonner? Eight thousand dollars would be a hell of a temptation, even to honest men."

Whit went over to the crowded bar and had to wait ten minutes before he could catch Doughbelly's eye and yell for a plug of chewing tobacco. When Doughbelly brought it his shirt was sticking to him and water ran off his face. He was smiling like a cat that has just caught a bird. He leaned far over the bar to say, "I hope those renegades don't show up for a week. It's not even Saturday, an' already I made as much as I'd make any two Saturdays." Doughbelly was summoned away southward by the thumping of thick-bottomed glasses atop his bar.

The crowd did not thin out much even though the small hours of the night rolled around, and the crisis that had brought them together in the first place had gotten more or less shunted aside in favor of a few poker games, some gossip swapping, and a little less drinking.

By the time Whit was ready to head for his cottage, Flaherty had departed to get a bed up at the rooming house, Sam Holt was no longer around and hadn't been for an hour or so, but the others did not particularly miss him because all he'd done had been whine about having one stage wrecked, a gun-guard killed, and the perils that were involved if he sent out other stages. Tom Hart went unsteadily across the dark roadway to his lean-to living quarters off the leather works, and Charley Bonner, who intended to sleep beside his desk up at the bank, with a shotgun beside him, walked out of the overheated saloon into a blast of late night—early morning—cold air.

Doughbelly eventually locked up. He studied the western horizon and was surprised that he was able to dimly make out the mountains. It was almost morning again. He went back to his quarters with his money drawer from the saloon, locked himself in, hid the drawer under an accumulation of unlaundered clothing, and went to bed.

As Whit was preparing to bed down he heard an occasional call among the patrolling vigilantes. He did not bother firing up the coal-oil lamp. Within moments of pulling up the blankets he was dead to the world.

*   *   *

There was some early-morning activity, but not within the vicinity of the saloon, the blacksmith's shop, the abstract office, the harness works or several other of the businesses whose proprietors had spent most of the night at the saloon.

The general store was open for business because the gimlet-eyed old gaffer who clerked for Walt Coggins had a key, but Walt did not show up.

Whit took a threadbare gray towel and a chunk of brown soap, and went trudging up the alley as far the barber's shop, paid two bits and had the bathhouse to himself for half an hour, after which he returned to his cottage, heard someone up front warping steel around an anvil—which meant that Wes had finally arrived at his smithy—and got dressed in clean attire, shaved, and went up to the café.

It was a short hike but long enough for Whit to observe the change in Beaverton. As old Flaherty had surmised last night would be the case, Beaverton resembled an armed outpost. By daylight, the lack of activity was very apparent. A few women with mesh shopping bags were moving through, mostly in the direction of Coggins's store, but there was no roadway traffic, although a mile or so north of town a freight wagon was approaching, and bulletproof steel shutters were in place to protect a number of glass windows.

At the café, because it was too late for breakfast, the jovial caféman was sitting on a high stool leaning across his counter reading a ragged old newspaper. When Whit walked in he very carefully folded his paper, tucked it away, and said, "I seen you at the waterin' hole last night. You look better than most of the fellers who was up there last an' been in here for breakfast today." He slid off his stool. "Ham, spuds, eggs, and java?"

Whit nodded and sat at the empty counter. From his cooking area the caféman called out. "If I was Jesse James and wanted to raid a town, I'd pick Beaverton this morning. Even the ones who wasn't drunk up there last night slept in this morning like a bunch of denned-up bears. Look out there. You could shoot a damned cannon from one end of town clean out the other end and not hit a damned thing, not even a dog."

Whit did not turn to look out the window. He sat in silence, waiting to be fed. As the caféman brought his coffee and platter he wagged his head. "You think it might be true that Mister Bonner's got fifty thousand dollars in his vault?"

Whit's poised fork stopped in midair. He remembered the blacksmith mentioning a guerilla band of fifteen renegades yesterday in Hart's shop. "Where did you hear that?" he asked, and allowed the caféman no time to answer. "The figure I heard Bonner give was eight thousand dollars."

The caféman probably had not believed the larger amount because he simply shrugged fleshy shoulders. "Still a lot of money, ain't it?"

Whit nodded his head and went to work on his first meal of the day. The caféman returned to his cooking area, which was partitioned off from the counter by a curtain that had very improbable, huge red cabbage roses printed on it.

Whit finished, paid up, and walked out front. Northward on the opposite side of the road two men carrying Winchesters were conversing in plain sight in front of Doctor Muller's place, which was his combination cottage and two-bed hospital.

He crossed over to the harness works, and Tom raised slightly bleary eyes from behind his counter where he was placing a tin template atop a rolled-out cowhide on his cutting table. He said, "Morning. Or is it afternoon? The pot's hot." He gestured toward his popping old wood-stove and went back to work.

Whit did not go after coffee; he leaned on the counter, concentrating on skiving off an after-breakfast sliver of molasses-cured, which he tongued into his cheek before pocketing the plug and clasp knife.

He watched Tom moving his saddle-skirt template from one place to another so that he could make the cut where it would leave the most leather to be used for other cuts. Tom halted, straightened up, and said, "Sam's runnin' around, wringin' his hands. He sent out the morning coaches this morning an' he came in here to tell me he expected both of them to be ambushed and robbed."

"What was on them?" Whit asked.

Tom leaned on the counter looking out into the sun-bright empty roadway. "Two traveling peddlers on the southbound and some freight on the northbound." Tom turned slowly back around. "He ought to be in the cattle business—he's real good at worrying."

"Have you seen Charley Bonner today?"

Tom snorted. "No, an' I don't expect to. I doubt that he'll even poke his snoot out the front door when it's time to eat."

"Does he still have some men in the bank with him?"

"I got no idea, and today I wouldn't walk up to that front door of his if I had a thousand dollars to put up in deposit. My guess is that he's got a small army in there with him. That's how he was talkin' last night."

Whit turned slightly so he could see the roadway. Usually, there was dust stirring out there. Today there was no dust and none of the kinds of vehicles and shod animals that raised it.

He left Tom Hart's shop to cross to the opposite side of the road and walk northward until there were empty places between buildings so he could see the westerly flow of open country.

He did not expect to see any mirrors reflecting light to warn the town that the outlaws had been sighted, so he wasn't disappointed when he didn't see any.

Sam Holt had seen him pass and left the corralyard to cross over and walk up where Whit was standing under the overhang of the gunsmith's shop. He called a greeting before getting up very close, and when Whit responded without looking away from the westerly distance, Sam halted to also look out there, then removed his glasses and went to work polishing them on a big blue bandanna as he said, "The morning stage came in a couple hours back from up north." Sam paused to hook the glasses into place and pocket his bandanna. "The driver didn't have any trouble or see any sign of three riders."

Whit gazed at Holt. "They wouldn't be ridin' in plain sight that far north, Sam. Unless they wasn't comin' this way at all."

"The lady on the stage said she seen some rangemen about two miles above town."

"Just riding?"

"No. Trying to bunch some cattle they'd got up out of a draw. The drummer who was on the same coach didn't even see that much. I think he was sleepin' one off though, because when I talked to him his breath would have gagged a buzzard. He's down at Walt's store by now. He handles bolt goods, women's shoes, and the like."

Whit jettisoned his cud, gave up on looking for mirror flashes, and started down toward Doughbelly's saloon. Sam went as far as the spindle doors with him, then veered off in the direction of his corralyard.

12

Rising Fears

OLD Flaherty bought a shearing and a shave at the tonsorial parlor, listened to the talkative barber until he knew about as much about conditions in town as anyone else, paid up, and went outside smelling elegantly of lilac-scented French toilet water. He met Doctor Muller, who had recently returned to town from a long buggy ride to a stump ranch where some eggs-and-goat-people were breaking their hearts, trying to squeeze a living out of a hundred and sixty acres they'd bought sight unseen from a railroad land office somewhere back east.

He had delivered a baby out there, hadn't been fed afterward and, by the time he encountered Mike Flaherty, had been on his way to the café, hungry as a bitch wolf. He stopped to listen briefly to what Flaherty had just heard from the barber, then went on down to the café.

An hour later when he got back up to his residence he had a patient waiting, a slim, intense young woman with dark eyes and curly dark hair. She told him she had either broken her right arm or had sprained it badly alighting from the stagecoach down at the corralyard.

Muller examined the arm, which was swollen, pronounced the injury a sprain, not a break, and advised the handsome young woman to wear the arm in a sling for about a week or until the swelling went down, but she was afraid of bumping the arm and asked to have it properly bandaged as an added protection.

The doctor complied, although he told her it really was not that serious an injury. Afterward she thanked him with a smile he had a little difficulty forgetting, and paid him five dollars, about twice what he got for splinting a broken arm.

He was rummaging for cigars in a desk drawer when the town blacksmith arrived with a badly gashed left forearm. Muller listened to the angry, profane explanation as he examined the injury, and when the blacksmith stopped swearing, Muller sat back, plugged a stogie into his mouth, and said, "You know your business better'n I do, Wes, but all the same I'm going to pass on to you something my uncle told me years ago. He did blacksmithing too. He said when a man has a hoof ready to nail a shoe onto, if he don't know the animal, he wants to drive in the first nail and make the clinch real fast, otherwise the horse can lunge, pull his hoof free, and, in doing that, will drag the unclinched sharp end of the nail across his arm and make a wound like you got here."

The blacksmith got red in the face, but said nothing until his arm was flushed clean, dressed, and bandaged. Then, as he arose to dig some silver from a trouser pocket he fixed Carl with a sulphurous look and said, "An' when your uncle's horse yanks free with just one nail holdin' the shoe, he flips it sideways, bends the shoe, and when you get him cross-tied again you got to spend an extra ten minutes at the forge an' anvil straightenin' out the confounded shoe."

Muller considered the blacksmith in silence for a moment, pocketed the silver coins, and escorted him to the front door. As he was watching the blacksmith trudge southward across the road he said, "Pig-headed old goat. Next time it'll be a kick up alongside your thick head."

The doctor cleaned up his little examination room, relit his stogie, and crossed to his office to write in his journal. He had kept a daily record of his professional activities for quite a few years, since his wife had died. She had done that for him and had encouraged him to continue even after she went to bed with the lingering illness that eventually took her life.

He did this because in some way it made him feel closer to her, not because he particularly cared whose arm he splinted, whose arm was gashed by a horseshoe nail, or whose kid fell out of a tree and cracked his collarbone.

Doctor Muller wasn't the only widower in town. Tom Hart was also a widower, and it was rumored that Doughbelly Price had buried a wife back in Missouri. If there was a difference among the Beaverton widowers it could have been that Carl Muller, being an educated, circumspect, and orderly individual, accepted loneliness more introspectively and broodingly than either the saloonman or the harness maker, both of whom were not cursed with long memories or great depths of sentimental feeling.

When he finished in the office, Muller put on his hat and coat, locked up out front, and struck out toward the center of town. A lanky, graying man cradling a Winchester in his arms was standing indolently with his back to a storefront and nodded as the doctor passed.

When he got down as far as the leather works he halted to lift out his watch and consult it, then repocket it, glancing across at the brick bank building. The man who operated the livery barn at the lower end of town emerged from the harness shop, saw Muller, and said, "Doctor, them horses of mine you fellers hired a few days back an' never returned is still bein' charged to all of you by the day."

Muller eyed the liveryman. "You'll get them back as soon as someone from town can ride out there and bring them back. Right now—"

A keening, high call rang out from somewhere behind town to the west. There were no words, just the yell. It struck both Muller and the liveryman as a cry of warning. The liveryman went toward the lower end of town in a very rapid walk. Carl Muller hesitated for a moment, then walked briskly in the direction of an empty space between two buildings. Behind him, Tom Hart called out, "Who was that? You see anything, Carl?"

Muller did not look back or reply; he started through the refuse-littered vacant space. When he reached the alley Tom caught up. They halted out there, looking left and right. The yell had not been repeated, but as they stood there, Sam Holt appeared up the alley northward, out behind his palisaded corralyard. Tom called and Sam pointed with a rigid arm, then ducked back through a little gate into his corralyard.

Four horsemen were distantly visible against the far mountains. Northward, two other horsemen were loping toward the stage road. They were closer. Hart said, "That's Sam's new gun-guard. That one out front. I can't make out the rider behind him." Tom tugged Carl's sleeve. "They signaled, sure as hell. They saw those four riders and signaled, and someone here in town saw the flash and yelled a warning."

Muller's cigar was dead in his mouth. He methodically relighted it, removed it, and watched Buffler Stoneman and his companion reach the roadway and turn southward toward town in a lope. He spat, plugged the stogie back into place, and turned around to watch the distant riders as he spoke from the side of his mouth. "Go round 'em up, Tom. Pass the warning. No one's to be out in the roadway, no womanfolk or kids on Main Street at all. Tell Whit and Wes to get the vigilantes hid on both sides of the road. Go on."

Hart left the medical practitioner standing in the alley, watching the southwesterly distance and trying to make an estimate as to how long it had taken the renegades to cross the rims, get down the far side, and ride up this close to town.

All he or anyone else could really make out was that four horsemen were coming toward town—with the forested dark mountains as a backdrop that made any kind of detailed examination impossible.

Carl had to relight the cigar again. As he was doing this he heard men calling behind him in the direction of Main Street. When he had another head of smoke rising from the stogie, he moved back to a picket fence and leaned there, watching the horsemen.

If they turned out to be someone's range riders, or maybe a band of hunters heading for town for supplies, and made the mistake of stopping to tie up out front of the bank, Beaverton could very well be remembered years from now as the place where a town full of agitated people had committed wholesale murder.

Muller flung down the cigar and went back through the overgrown and trash-littered open ground toward the center of town.

A slab-sided, bony-tailed brindle dog went sniffing along in the roadway close to the opposite plankwalk. Otherwise there was no movement, but Carl saw men hovering in dog trots, carbines up and ready, hidden in recessed doorways, waiting over at Coggins's store and elsewhere. He saw Whit Pierson and Tom Hart out front of the harness works. Neither had a carbine but both wore shellbelts and sidearms. He started toward them.

The burly gun-guard who worked for Sam Holt emerged from the corralyard, walking southward. The man who had returned to town with him was nowhere in sight.

About the time Carl Muller reached Tom and Whit, the gun-guard also got down there. He did not wait to be questioned. "We seen 'em just as they was breakin' clear of the timber. We didn't signal until they was far enough ahead so's we could be sure it was four riders. Then we signaled and headed for town."

Whit had a question. "Did they see you?"

Buffler Stoneman shook his head. "Naw. They couldn't even see the mirror flash, it was made toward town, not toward them. An' they was too far off to see much else, except maybe a couple of rangemen headin' toward town from up north."

Stoneman looked across the road, looked back smiling. "You remember what happened to the Daltons up in Minnesota? They rode into a town where everyone was waitin' for them just like is happenin' here."

Carl Muller spoke slowly, almost stolidly. "Just a minute. I'm not saying it isn't them, it probably is, but the whole town is holding its breath with fingers curled around triggers. If it happens to be strangers passing through, or maybe some riders from one of the distant cow outfits . . . If they happen to have business at the bank and tie up out front, they're never going to know what hit them."

Tom and Whit gazed steadily at the doctor, but Stoneman made a derisive snort. "Nobody in his right mind will tie up in front of the bank today."

"Except strangers," stated Carl Muller, and let that lie there through a moment of silence. Stoneman glanced at Whit and Tom; they were still watching Muller's face. Stoneman flapped his arms and started to leave. Whit said, "Wait a minute."

The burly man turned, eyeing Whit testily. "What d'you want to do, ride out an' meet 'em wavin' a white flag?" he asked.

Whit ignored the sarcasm. "We got a problem, Buffler. None of us have seen those outlaws up close. We got no idea what they look like. You go tell Sam Holt not to do a damned thing until someone's had a chance to make damned sure who they are."

Stoneman stood gazing steadily at Whit until Doctor Muller stepped ahead, took Stoneman by the arm, and said, "I'll go with you." The burly, bearded man turned his back on Whit Pierson and walked northward.

Tom Hart said, "He wasn't real happy."

Whit ignored that, jerked his head for Tom to follow along, and struck out for the alley. When they got there, they discovered that along the full length of the alley, beginning at the north end of Beaverton and continuing all the way southward to the lower end, there were armed men standing like statues, not making a sound, standing at irregular intervals with their Winchesters, watching the slow-gaited approach of four riders with the sun in their faces and the mountains far off in the background.

Whit approached the big, rough blond man who worked for the town blacksmith. The blond man turned, wearing a wolfish expression. "They ain't goin' to reach Main Street," he told Whit.

"If they're riders from one of those foothill cow outfits . . . ," Whit said, and did not finish the sentence. He and the big apprentice blacksmith looked straight at one another for a long time, until the blond man grounded his Winchester, looked up and down the alley at the other watchers, and furrowed his brow at Whit. "An' supposin' it ain't? Supposin' it's them outlaws?"

Tom Hart put in his two-bits' worth. "They got Marshal Given for a shield. They'll have him out front. You start a war and you're goin' to nail him sure as hell."

The blond man's expression changed slowly. Whit took advantage of this. "Pass the word up an' down the alley. No shooting back here. Let them ride past and enter town. We've passed the word up an' down Main Street to do the same thing. Let 'em get into town."

The blond man grounded his Winchester and leaned on it regarding Pierson and the harness maker. "All right. But I don't know about Wes. He's holed up over at the smithy, hopin' they come into town from the south so's he can open up on 'em ahead of everyone else."

"You just make sure no one in this alley opens up on them," Whit said, beginning to turn back the way he had come. "We'll talk to Wes."

Tom was slow in following because he had been squinting in the direction of those distant but steadily advancing riders. When he caught up with Whit on Main Street he said, "That didn't look like Jack Given in the lead."

Whit continued in the direction of the smithy as he replied. "How the hell can you tell that when they're so far off, Tom?"

"Well, I couldn't, only Jack sets straight in the saddle."

"You couldn't make that out from here," scoffed Whit, as they turned into the open-fronted, heavily soot-blackened blacksmith shop.

There was no one there. They went through the place, even went out back where they could see Whit Pierson's little house, but they did not find the blacksmith.

Tom returned to the open front of the structure, looking northward up through town. He called Whit and said, "In the general store. I just saw four fellers go in there. If Wes isn't down here, he's most likely up there."

13

Mounting Tensions

HART'S guess was correct, but the blacksmith wasn't the only person in the store. Walt Coggins was behind his counter, selling boxes of bullets about as fast as he could take them off a shelf, and like everyone else he was wearing a sidearm.

The town barber was carrying a long-barreled military rifle; even the grumpy old man who ran the abstract office was there with a hogleg six-shooter shoved into his waistband and a Sharp's trapdoor carbine in his hands. He and Mike Flaherty were standing along the counter in front of the bolt goods, both smoking cigars and occasionally grumbling something to each other.

Flaherty saw Tom Hart and Whit enter, and worked through the noisy crowd to meet them with a hard little humorless smile. "If you boys come to buy bullets you better hurry." Flaherty gestured behind at the loudly talking crowd of townsmen. "If we'd had this kind of cooperation twenty years ago we wouldn't have needed no army out here to chase the In'ians out of the country." Flaherty dropped his arm, puffed a moment, then shook his head. "Three raggedy-pantsed outlaws—a man would think the Rebel army was coming."

Several townsmen started for the door. Whit moved ahead to bar their passage. He yelled for silence and got it. Even Walt Coggins was staring at him as Whit said, "No one fires a weapon until we're damned certain those are the renegades."

The blacksmith challenged that. "Yeah? An' how are you goin' to do that? You know 'em by sight?"

"No, we don't know them by sight and they've never seen us either, but if those riders come into town with Marshal Given out front, some of you gents can get up at the north end of town on both sides of the road, and when they ride past, you can close off that way back out of town."

The old man who owned the abstract office had a sarcastic question. "Why should we take any chances with this bunch?" Several others nodded and mumbled agreement.

Whit answered, "What if the riders are pothunters headin' to town for supplies? Or maybe just some traveling men who picked the wrong day to pass through?" The silence that followed this was total. Whit relaxed a little. "Pick hiding places if you want to, but don't start it. Leave that up to them, an' be careful about Marshal Given."

Coggins frowned. "Who is going to challenge them, Whit?"

No one said a word. Tom Hart looked down his nose at all those heavily armed individuals who had been loudly saying what they would do to the outlaws ten minutes earlier. "I will," he said, and turned to leave the store and stand out front until Whit eventually joined him as men departed from Coggins's store to look for strategic places of concealment. Tom spat into the roadway. "Somebody's goin' to get killed," he told Whit, "an it don't have to be the marshal or them men he's ridin' with. Look—you never saw so many men with guns in one place before in your life. All it'll take is for one idiot to fire, an' they'll start shootin' from all directions. Whit, if a man had a lick of sense he'd go home, bar the door, and lie flat on the floor."

Sam Holt crossed from the opposite side of the road, carrying a Winchester in the crook of his arm and wearing a belt gun. He had his hat tipped low to protect his glasses from sun glare.

Tom eyed him scathingly. "There's a prime example," he

said in half a whisper before Holt reached them. "He couldn't hit a bull in the butt from fifty feet."

Holt nodded at them without smiling. "I just came from the alley. They're no more'n a mile an' a half out." Sam paused, then said, "An' Jack Given is riding in front beside a heavyset feller with a full beard an' a carbine across the saddle in his lap."

Tom scowled. "You saw all that, Sam, with them a mile away?"

"No. Doughbelly's got a brass spyglass. He's over there with it."

Whit blew out a long breath and turned to watch townsmen fading from sight on both sides of Main Street at the northernmost end of town. He looked elsewhere and saw more armed men in places of concealment. Up in front of the bank there was no one in sight, but there were dog-trots on both sides of the brick building. Tom guessed armed men were out of sight in those narrow places.

The steel shutters on the bank's two front windows were closed. The building seemed isolated from the other activity. Whit imagined Charley in there, sweating like a stud horse, his hired gunhands sweltering in the half-darkness. Another time he would have smiled, but not now.

Sam Holt walked in the direction of the saloon, with Tom Hart caustically watching him. He was turning to speak when someone across the road called out. "They stopped out yonder. They're settin' their horses and lookin' over here."

Whit and Hart struck out. By the time they reached the alley most of the armed men had discreetly sought places of concealment, but Doughbelly was still there, leaning on a post with his spyglass to his face. He did not look around until Tom Hart asked if he was sure Marshal Given was out there. Doughbelly turned a little. "Yeah. Here, balance it atop the post otherwise it'll move. Jack's beside that older feller with the whiskers."

Tom had to bend down to use the spyglass. For a long

moment he squinted, shifted slightly and made a wider scan, then he grunted, handed the spyglass to Whit, and blew out a big breath as he addressed the saloonman. "Yeah. It's Jack an' he don't look too good."

"If you was in his boots you wouldn't neither," retorted Doughbelly, accepting his spyglass from Whit and moving back to the post to resume his vigil.

Whit was whittling off a chew when he and the harness maker exchanged a look.

Doughbelly suddenly spoke. "Hey! They're startin' up again. Anglin' toward the upper end of town." Doughbelly pulled back, considered the position of the sun, then resumed his position with the spyglass. As Whit was turning away, the saloonman said, "Maybe they sense somethin' is wrong. They're fannin' out a little an' they're not talkin' now, they're watchin' things over here."

Whit went back to Main Street, sent Hart northward to warn the men waiting at the upper end of town, then crossed to Coggins's store to pass the word that the waiting would be over shortly. Within the next half hour or so.

From this point on, as word spread that the showdown was imminent, the loud talk ceased, as did most of the movement on both sides of the road. Walt Coggins walked out front, chewing a cigar. He was watching the northern end of town when he spoke to Whit.

"The bank might be the best place to be today. It's awful quiet up there. But Charley will be watching."

Carl Muller came along to announce that Tom Hart and Pete were on the roof of the rooming house. Carl sniffed. "Snipers. I'm beginning to feel sorry for those idiots. Maybe they'll scent trouble and turn back."

"They're coming," stated Whit, and Doctor Muller looked morosely at him. "It'll be like a shooting gallery."

Coggins shrugged his beefy shoulders. "Don't feel too sorry for them, Carl. They didn't give Dan Crockett a chance. You said he'd been shot in the back. And they'll kill the marshal, for sure."

Muller delved for his pocket watch, considered its little hands, and as he was pocketing it he said, "Any strangers in town now are going to get an impression of Beaverton they'll never forget."

Coggins chewed his stogie while considering the doctor. "We didn't start this, Carl. An' there can't be many strangers around anyway because Sam's stages aren't due in town for some time yet."

Muller raised his eyes to the storekeeper's face. "I was thinking of one, Charley. A pretty little fine-boned woman with a smile that'd melt stone. She came in this morning on the southbound, fell getting out, and sprained her arm. I bandaged it for her. It bothers me that she's goin' to see a massacre."

Coggins was watching the north end of town again and may not even have heard what Muller said. Whether he did or not, he made no reply.

One of the men from the alley came over to the edge of the opposite plankwalk and spoke without raising his voice. "They're gettin' set. The feller with the whiskers is takin' Marshal Given up around to the north roadway. The others is comin' straight in from the west so as one of 'em'll pass through from across the alley near the lower end of town. The other one is comin' straight toward the middle of town. That one's goin' to ride between the houses and shacks and reach the alleyway."

Coggins said, "How far out?"

"Less than a mile," the townsman said, and turned back toward the part of the alley from which he had come.

Whit leaned, sprayed amber, straightened back, and looked northward. "If they wasn't ridin' into a trap, they might pull it off. Whiskers will approach the bank with the marshal. The other two will set their horses back out of sight a little ways across the road to shoot at anyone who gets curious up by the bank."

Coggins returned to his store and Doctor Muller looked away from Whit as Sam Holt walked up behind them. Holt said, "They'll know somethin' is wrong the minute they get close enough to see Main Street. It's empty, the town's as quiet as a grave, an' anyone with half an eye will be able to see gun muzzles here and there."

Whit said, "It will be too late, Sam. They'll have armed men behind them and facing them."

Carl Muller's mood hadn't improved as he faced the stage company's owner. "I hope they give up when they see what they're up against. I expect that pretty little dark-eyed lady has a room up at the rooming house, and if it's facing the road . . . Women hadn't ought to see things like this."

Sam Holt removed his glasses to polish them as he said, "What lady are you talkin' about, Carl?"

"Pretty, slight-built young one with black curly hair and dark eyes, who came in on your stage from up north this morning and slipped getting out and sprained her arm."

Holt finished with the glasses, hooked them back into place, and stared at Doctor Muller. "Oh, her. She didn't slip an' hurt herself gettin' out of the stage."

Doctor Muller gazed stonily back at Sam Holt. "I bandaged her arm, Sam, and I know a sprain when I see one. She thought the arm was broken. It probably hurt like it was, but it was a sprain and the arm was swollen."

Holt's eyes looked oversized behind his spectacles. "Carl, damn it all, I was standin' right there when they unloaded some light freight from the boot. I wasn't ten feet from her when she got out. She did not slip an' fall."

Whit, half-listening to this discussion, saw someone atop the distant rooming house stand up and wave his hat. He wanted to swear. The riders approaching the upper end of town only had to be glancing around and upward to have seen that. "Damned fool," he snarled in a tone of voice that brought the arguing men around staring at him.

He gestured. "That darned Mexican on the rooming-house roof stood up and waved his hat. I expect he was signaling that they are getting closer.

Holt and Muller looked northward, but there was no longer any sign of anyone on the roof.

This time when a man from the alley appeared across the road, he did not say a word; he gestured with his Winchester to an area between the livery barn and the more northerly abstract office where there was an empty parcel of ground. Whit nudged his companions and stepped toward the recessed doorway of the general store.

The wait was over.

Whit sank to one knee and leaned to watch the upper end of town. Behind him, Holt faded back inside the store, heading for the rear doorway. He entered the alley on the east side of town, walking southward, down to where one of the outlaws was expected to arrive on the opposite side of the road.

Carl Muller did nothing. He seemed preoccupied. Behind him several townsmen crept forward to crowd around in the doorway where they peeked northward too.

Whit finally saw what they had all been waiting for: two mounted men rode up over the east-side berm to reach the road and rein southward. One of them was Marshal Jack Given. The other one was the thickly built, bearded man Whit would have bet new money was the same man who had snarled at the youngest outlaw back up among those pock-marked lava boulders.

Whit briefly switched his attention toward the bank building. It was exactly as it had been for some time, absolutely silent, formidably barred at door and windows, like an impregnable fortress. It put Whit in mind of the Alamo. He spat before returning his attention to Jack Given and the outlaw he was riding with. They were less than a hundred yards from the northernmost end of Beaverton where buildings on both sides of the road stood shoulder to shoulder. There would be only one way for that outlaw to flee—if he got spooked—straight down Main Street toward the southern end of town. And there was not even a remote possibility that he could survive a ride like that with armed men concealed on both sides of the road, itching to use their weapons.

Doctor Muller roused from his reverie and looked around. "Where did Sam go?" he asked. No one answered.

Every eye in town was fixed on the two horsemen just now entering town from the north.

14

Springing the Trap

THE bearded outlaw said something to Marshal Given and yanked his horse to a halt. They sat up there as motionless as stones. Someone whispered in Whit's ear, an unnecessary precaution. "He's figurin' it's a trap."

Whit did not acknowledge the remark. He was watching the outlaw intently. So was everyone else. Marshal Given was slouching in the saddle, looking dog-tired.

The burly outlaw had a carbine balanced across his lap. He was holding it with his right hand. He said something to the marshal and slowly turned his head from side to side. Whit was scarcely breathing.

Doctor Muller said, "Murder, plain and simple." He had no sooner spoken than a voice as dry as old corn husks called to the outlaw from the rooming-house roof. "Drop the Winchester and set real still."

The burly man raised his face very slowly, searching for whoever had spoken. There was no one up there for him to see. Marshal Given did not look up, but he said something that made his captor raise the carbine slightly in his lap with the barrel less than four feet from Given's right side. Then he spoke, loud enough to be heard on the roof but not quite loud enough to be heard much farther.

"Listen to me, up there. We're goin' to turn an' ride back out of here the way we come, an' if you try anythin', your marshal is goin' to get killed. You hear me?"

There was no reply from the rooftop. The outlaw gave

Marshal Given an order. "Turn, slow now, an' ride out of here. An' you better pray, mister. Real hard." The outlaw cocked his Winchester as he kneed his horse around to be on Jack Given's far side. "Just slow an' easy," he said, inching his animal close enough so that their stirrups bumped.

As they were moving back northward the outlaw raised his face and called to the men on the roof. "If you so much as cough up there, he's a dead son of a bitch."

Someone elbowed his way to the front of the recessed doorway where Whit was crouching, knelt in plain sight of the upper roadway, and snugged back a rifle. As his head came down to align the sights Whit struck the gun aside and glared. "I'll blow your damned head off!"

Carl Muller leaned, grasped the gun, and wrenched it out of its owner's hands.

But that was not where the fight started. The outlaw and Jack Given were leaving town by the stage road when down near the opposite end of Beaverton someone yelled and fired a gun. That was all that was needed. Gunfire broke out.

As Carl Muller had predicted, it was like a shooting gallery. The bearded outlaw reined sharply southward toward the lower end of town. He fired his Winchester once, at someone behind him, dropped it and yanked out his six-gun. He snapped wild shots as he roweled his horse so hard it sprang ahead in a wild jump and landed in a belly-down race toward the south roadway out of town.

The horse was in mid-air when bullets struck him. He folded his legs in the air and was dead before he came down in a compact fall that might have ended like that except for the momentum that made him go completely end over end, like a cartwheel, with bullet-dust blossoming around him from both sides of Main Street.

His rider was hit but landed on his feet, somehow avoided being struck as the horse went completely over, and was twisting to get farther away when the gunfire cut him down and rolled him in spasmodic jerks.

Then someone down at either the blacksmith's shop or across from it at the livery barn began firing at the other two outlaws, who had entered town from the lower end and had sat their saddles back a few yards from the roadway, where they could watch the front of the bank. When guns fired from all over town these two tried the same method of escape, with pretty much the same results. One died in the first round of bullets.

Someone yelled and fired a deep, thunderous shot that killed the other outlaw's horse before it could swing southward. Its rider was knocked flat. Bullets were searching the dust for him as he got up into a low crouch and ran blindly in the direction of the livery barn. He drew his six-gun as he zigzagged, but did not fire it.

He almost made it, which was a miracle in itself. It sounded as though everyone on both sides of the road was firing at him. Someone in the livery barn with a big-bored old trap-door rifle squeezed off another shot. The slug jolted the running outlaw straight up to his full height before he collapsed, dead.

Whit had not fired a shot. Neither had Coggins nor Carl Muller, but the townsmen crowding into the store's doorway had nearly deafened Whit with their uninterrupted gunfire.

Whit arose and moved out to the plankwalk, looking northward. Two riderless horses were heading straight up the road, stirrups flapping, reins broken off short from being stepped on.

Four sprawling men were in the settling dust, a few hundred yards apart. One was trying to move. It was the marshal. He would push upward and claw in the dirt, only to collapse again. Whit looked around as someone pushed roughly past. It was Doctor Muller heading up there.

Several men walked out into the roadway. Among them was Sam Holt. They stood above the first outlaw to die. Farther down Main Street other men emerged from places of concealment to walk out and look at the other two dead men, among them the dour old man who owned the abstract office. He grounded his old army-issue weapon and leaned on it, shaking his head. He had scored twice, but other bullets had also hit the sprawling outlaw lying dead in the center of the road. It had nevertheless been the slug from his big-bored gun that had killed the man.

Mike Flaherty nudged the old man. "What'd you have that thing loaded with, grapeshot?"

The old man acted deaf. After a while he raised his gun, flipped it open, ejected the large brass casing, and dropped it on the dead outlaw. Then he looked at Flaherty. "He wasn't no more'n eighteen, nineteen years old."

Flaherty gazed coldly at the corpse. "Old enough to pull a trigger."

The old man shouldered his trapdoor weapon, turned away, and went trudging in the direction of the abstract office. Flaherty lost interest too. He looked around, saw the gathering crowd at the north end of town and started walking up there.

The roadway was full of armed men, mostly talking or yelling back and forth, but a few had gone back to the plankwalks and were standing there, eyeing the carnage. Doughbelly was among them. As Mike Flaherty went past, Doughbelly called out and started after him. Flaherty waited, nodded brusquely, and started forward again. Doughbelly glanced in the direction of his saloon as they passed it, and licked his lips. Two thirds of the way along he said, "That was like a war."

Flaherty's flinty gaze was fixed on the crowd in the roadway north of town when he replied to that. "Naw. More like a massacre . . . An' I'm out two good horses."

By the time they reached the crowd above town, a stretcher-blanket had been made for someone up there, with men holding it taut on both sides as they were led by Doctor Muller down in the direction of his cottage.

Flaherty and Doughbelly gave them plenty of room in the

center of the road. They both saw the limply unconscious and bloody man on the blanket, but only Doughbelly reacted. "Jack! Marshal Given for crissake!"

Flaherty eyed the blanket as it moved past, pursed his lips and said nothing. He had seen his share of dead men. It was his private opinion that if the man being carried away wasn't dead, he damned well soon would be.

Whit came along, walking with Tom Hart, both of them carrying carbines and looking solemn. Doughbelly said, "What happened up here, Tom?"

The harness maker growled. "When the fight started southward, that furry-faced son of a bitch shot Jack. He was riding real close with his carbine slanted across his lap."

"Is he dead?"

Hart shook his head. "No. Doc didn't say much, but there was blood everywhere, like someone had been butcherin' hogs. How about those other two?"

"Shot all to hell," stated Flaherty, "an' my two horses they was ridin', to boot." Flaherty jutted his jaw up where men completely obscured the other body in the north roadway. "How about him?"

Hart's reply was crisp. "From the top of the rooming house I aimed between his shoulderblades and blew half his head off."

Flaherty accepted this. "It's always hard to hit what a man's aimin' at when he's up above it shootin' downwards. Anyone know who they were?"

Whit was watching the stretcher bearers crowding through Muller's little picket gate. "No. Maybe they'll have something in their pockets. Otherwise Jack'll maybe be able to tell us. But that might be a while—if ever."

He left them walking toward Muller's cottage. Doughbelly forced lightness to his voice when he said, "Drinks are on me for the first round, gents."

Flaherty gestured. "Who's goin' to clean up the mess down there?"

Tom Hart was already moving toward the saloon when he replied. "Not us. We didn't do any shootin' down there."

They were the first to reach the saloon, but not long after their arrival other men drifted in, some still carrying rifles and carbines, all still wearing belt guns.

Doughbelly was as busy as a straw in a whirlwind. There was not much talk. That would come later, after a few hours had passed and enough popskull went down gullets to loosen tongues. At this point recollections were too vivid.

The saloon filled up gradually. Some of the late arrivals had blood on their shirts and trousers. They leaned at the bar, looking blankly ahead as Doughbelly poured their whiskey and left them alone.

It was Beaverton's old men, trailing in shortly before sunset, mostly widowers who lived in slab shacks at the lower end of town and who spent most of their days playing toothpick poker near the front window of the saloon, who got the talk started.

Doughbelly took a bottle of dregs and glasses to their window table and was hastening back when one of them said, "Did you see Mister Holt hit one of them chains holdin' the sign over the blacksmith's shop when the firin' commenced?"

Doughbelly stopped. Holt had been on the same side of the road as the blacksmith's shop, and that hanging sign was twelve feet from the ground. From up the bar a dry voice said, "Yeah. I was standin' beside him. An' he shot out half the winders across the road."

One of the old gaffers laughed, showing toothless, wet gums. "I seen it too. The recoil knocked his glasses off. He got down all fours lookin' for them with the war goin' on above him. Doughbelly, you belong to the town posse, tell me suthin'. Does Mister Holt belong to your posse?"

The old man received no reply as Doughbelly returned to his bar where patrons were thumping the bartop for refills. Tom Hart reached for a bottle, refilled his jolt glass, and leaned to do the same for Whit. As he was putting the bottle aside he said, "Anybody take the saddlebags off them dead horses?"

Mike Flaherty was farther up the bar. He leaned to look down at the harness maker. "The storekeeper an' some older feller wearin' black sleeve protectors. I saw him in the store, so I expect he works for Mister Coggins." Flaherty continued to gaze down the bar. "They got a vault at the store?"

Hart nodded. "Yeah, in the back room. They'll be safe there."

Flaherty thought briefly about that before speaking again. "Maybe. But it'd most likely be better to put it 'em in the vault up at the bank."

No one disputed this. In fact, no one commented about it at all, but a few minutes later several townsmen left, presumably to get the saddlebags and take them up to the bank, but no one was very interested, least of all Whit and Hart, who were beginning to feel loose and comfortable. The stolen money would be in those saddlebags, and since the outlaws had not been where they could spend any of it since stealing it off the stage, it would all be there.

Whit finally looked up at the older man beside him. "Did you see it when the outlaw shot Jack?"

Hart hadn't been looking in that direction. He had been peeking southward where all the gunfire had abruptly erupted. "No. I got distracted when all hell busted loose southward. When I turned back, Pete was hollering something I couldn't hear. He was pointing too. That's when I saw Jack tryin' to get up after bein' shot and the outlaw startin' to run his horse. I shot him. Aimed for the middle of his back and liked to blown his damned head off."

A slightly breathless townsman came up and tapped Whit on the arm. "You better come," he said, keeping his voice low. "There's somethin' wrong up at the bank."

Whit stared at the man. So did Tom Hart. The eyes staring back were big and round. The man said, "We didn't go in."

"Then how do you know somethin' is wrong?"

"The door ain't barred from the inside. It's about half open and when we yelled in there for Mister Bonner, we didn't get no answer."

Whit and Tom started for the doorway with the nervous townsman following.

15

Some Red Faces

SOUTHWARD, the liveryman and two of his hostlers had a singletree chained to the rear legs of one of the dead horses. At the other end a pair of matched sorrels were hooked to the doubletree. When the liveryman whistled the sorrels leaned into their collars.

Except for this activity, the roadway was nearly empty. Mothers were keeping their children away from Main Street. In the direction of the bank the same feeling of isolation and deathly silence remained. Whit caught the harness maker's eye and shook his head.

As the townsman had said, the steel-reinforced oaken roadway door was hanging half open. Steel shutters were still in place along the front wall of the building. Inside, it was semidark, without a sound.

Whit threw out an arm to restrain Hart, who had his six-gun rising as he moved toward the door. He stopped. Whit motioned Hart to the opposite side of the doorway and flattened against his side. The townsman was back several yards, content to be an onlooker.

Whit raised his handgun as he called out. "Charley? Are you all right? Charley?"

There were echoes from inside the darkened building but no answers. Hart began to make gestures that Whit did not understand. Hart stopped gesturing and made one simple arm signal to indicate they should both jump inside at the same time.

Whit shook his head. He was a stage driver, not a hero. Hart rolled his eyes in exasperation as Whit removed his hat and sent it sailing inside. Nothing happened except that the harness maker gave Whit a scornful stare.

The townsman eased up to hand Whit a short scantling. Whit hefted the thing. It seemed to be part of a roughly milled two-by-four. He leaned and hurled it into the building. This time there was noise as the piece of wood struck objects, bounced, and struck other objects.

When silence returned, Tom was glaring darkly in the direction of the doorway when a slight scuffling sound came from inside. Tom called out. "Charley?"

The scuffling, rattling sound came again.

Whit knew what Tom would do, gripped his gun tighter, and cocked it. When the harness maker sprang ahead, Whit also moved inside.

They both fanned away from the doorway into deeper gloom and stopped to listen, to wait for their eyes to become accustomed to the change in light.

The rattling sound was repeated, more frantic this time. It seemed to be coming from inside the ornamental wooden railing that separated the bank's sacrosanct interior from the area used by customers.

Whit made certain Hart saw him and moved to the little gate in the railing, pushed past to the private area, and moved very slowly as he probed the darkness. The scuffling sound returned, definitely frantic this time. Whit went in the direction of the sound and stumbled against something soft and yielding. Immediately, the scuffling sound was loudly indignant.

Whit leaned, felt below his knees, encountered a man trussed like a turkey, and knelt to holster his weapon as he fished for his clasp knife.

Three slashes freed the man, who yanked furiously at the blue bandanna tied tightly around the lower part of his face. He was sweaty, hatless, and breathless as Whit helped him stand up, but the circulation had been impaired too long. The man groped for a chair and sank into it, making sounds like a landed whale.

Whit shook him by the shoulder. "Was it a robbery?"

The man stopped groaning long enough to nod. "Yes. Bonner's over by his desk somewhere. There are three other fellers somewhere in here. For crissake light a lamp, will you?"

Tom Hart came past the railing to take down one of the wall lamps and light it, lower the mantle, turn up the wick, and hook the thing back on its hanger as he turned slowly.

The other three guards Bonner had hired to help him protect the bank were also tied. One of them had a swelling on one side of his head with blood-clotted hair around it. When they got this man freed and into a chair he looked blearily at them and asked for whiskey. Hart sent the townsman, who had been standing beyond the railing, staring in shock, for some whiskey.

Charley Bonner had an angry, discolored swelling on one cheekbone, which gave his face a lopsided appearance. He stared glassy-eyed as Whit hoisted him to the chair at his desk and asked, "What happened?"

Bonner was a long time replying. His gaze went slowly around the room and ended up on the wide-open door of his big steel vault. In a voice so soft Whit barely heard it, he said, "Go look in the vault . . . Tell me what you see."

Whit was turning when one of the freed guards spoke in a bitter tone. "He ain't goin' to see nothing. After you got hit in the face and knocked out, Mister Bonner, she stepped over you and pulled the door wide open."

Whit and Hart stared at the speaker. Hart said, "*She*?"

The angry guard ignored that. "She made me'n Henry drag you over to your desk and tie you . . . Mister Bonner, why'd you let her in? You said when we locked ourselves inside you wasn't goin' to open that door for the Angel Gabriel."

Suddenly, the outer area of the bank was full of excited men. Hart snarled at several who would have pushed on into the private area. "Stay out there," he said to everyone except Doctor Muller. "Carl, you better look at 'em. They was tied for a long while and two of 'em been hurt."

The man who had gone for whiskey and who had announced in the saloon that it looked like the bank had been robbed, handed Tom Hart his bottle. Hart handed it to the seated man who had asked for whiskey.

The noise was annoying to Doctor Muller. He worked with it rising steadily as more townspeople crowded inside, but when it got to the point where he could not hear himself asking questions nor the answers he got back, he turned and yelled for everyone to clear out.

Beyond being surprised at his angry shout, and talking a little less, no one turned to depart. Tom Hart drew his handgun, pointed it, and said, "Out!"

That accomplished what the medical practicioner's exasperation had been unable to accomplish. One man remained, but he was already inside the railing helping with the freed guards. When some degree of order had been established, he removed his glasses and furiously polished them on a large blue bandanna, listening very intently to what was being said in the vicinity of Bonner's desk. He was a depositer, so his expression of personal anguish was justified as Charley Bonner explained how, about a half hour before all hell busted loose out in the roadway, someone had come along to rattle the roadway door. For a while he and others with him in there refused to even acknowledge the noise. Charley had given strict orders that neither the front nor back doors were to be opened no matter what.

The knocking became more insistent. Charley had finally gone over to the door to loudly say that the bank was closed. The answer he got back surprised everyone inside the bank. A woman had said her name was Elizabeth Harding, that she was a clerk at the Meadowville bank up north where that earlier shipment of money had come from, that she had another pouch of greenbacks destined for the army posts south of Livermore, and that she had been instructed to stay at the rooming house in Beaverton with the pouch and leave with it the following morning on the first southbound stage. After arriving in Beaverton and hearing the talk of an imminent raid by outlaws, she had decided to ask permission to put her money pouch in the Beaverton bank's vault.

When Charley finished speaking there was a long moment of silence. Except for the sullen guards, Charley's audience seemed willing to understand the banker's dilemma. When he said he had unbarred the door to admit the young woman with the large leather money pouch on her arm, one man said, "Which arm, Charley?"

The banker looked up. "Which arm? You mean which arm was she carrying the pouch on?"

Doctor Muller nodded his head without speaking or taking his eyes off the seated banker.

One of the guards answered gruffly. "The left arm. She had a cast on her right arm."

Carl turned slowly to gaze at Sam Holt, who had his glasses hooked back into place and was barely breathing. The doctor said, "You were right, Sam. She didn't fall getting out of a stage." He swung his attention to Whit and Tom. "When I bandaged her arm, believe me it was swollen. But she wouldn't be the first person to bruise themselves on purpose. And while I was bandaging the arm she kept her fist closed. When I asked her to open it she said it hurt more with the fingers extended, so I bandaged it with the fist closed." He felt inside his coat for a stogie, bit off the end, and said, "Charley, what kind of a gun was she holding?"

Again one of the disgruntled guards replied, "A double-action Colt Lightning with the barrel sawed off to about three inches, an' you're right, Doctor, she handed Mister Bonner the pouch an' we didn't even see her push the hand out holdin' that little gun until she hit Mister Bonner in the face an' he fell down."

Sam Holt started polishing his glasses again, with considerable vigor this time. Whit leaned against the railing, watching the whiskey bottle go around. When it came to Charley Bonner he waved it away and rummaged in a low desk drawer for a private bottle. He took two swallows and offered the bottle to Doctor Muller, who accepted it but did not drink from it. He handed it to Sam Holt, who did drink from it, three or four swallows.

One of the guards arose, tested his legs, then went over to the man with the clotted blood on the side of his head. He leaned, then spoke without turning around. "Doc, Art's got a nasty one."

Muller moved dutifully to the injured guard. As he raised the man's head to see the injury better he said, "She hit you too?"

"Yeah. She said she'd shoot every damned one of us if she had to, and told me to hold the pouch while Mister Bonner emptied the vault. Then she hit me after I handed her the pouch."

Charley was beginning to gain color. He said, "Art, did she get it all?"

The injured man had his eyes tightly closed from pain as Doctor Muller ungently pushed and pulled at his injury. "She must have hit you pretty hard, Mister Bonner. You put it all in the pouch I was holding."

Bonner raised his bottle again.

One of the guards asked what had happened in the roadway. Whit told him. The guard's mouth drooped. "Slicker'n a damned whistle. You know who she was? Naw, you wouldn't know. She was a clerk from the Meadowville bank all right. Just like she said. She also said she was the one who told them outlaws about the money comin' down here from up yonder. One of them outlaws was her close friend."

Everyone watched this man as he paused to tip up the

bottle and drain it before speaking again. He put the bottle atop a desk and gazed stonily at it. "The only reason I can figure for her to tell us all that was to let us know she'd use that damned gun. An' I sure as hell believed her. She's wasn't much bigger'n a schoolboy, but that gun made her seem ten feet tall."

"Did she leave by the front door?" Doctor Muller asked.

The guard shook his head, still staring at the empty bottle. "By the alley door. After she tied us like shoats. And for a little thing she was strong. She yanked them ropes as hard as a man could've done."

There was a period of silence during which Doctor Muller told the man with the bloody scalp he would have to come up to the cottage for a proper dressing.

Sam Holt went through to the rear of the building and returned. "That's how she left," he announced. "Door's gaping open."

Tom Hart started to ask if she'd had a horse back there, decided Sam wouldn't have seen the tracks if there had been any, and walked toward the rear door with Whit in his wake.

There were no fresh tracks, none that they could make out anyway, nor was there a place where a horse had been standing for any length of time. They would have found the sign if there had been.

Whit stood up to scratch his head. Daylight was waning over town, but in the east-side alleyway it had already turned to predusk shadows. "She left footprints," he told the harness maker.

Hart nodded. "I'll get a lantern."

Whit ignored that to say, "She arrived on a stage, roomed over at Pete's place, and came to the bank before the fight. Let's go down to the livery barn. She didn't escape by stage because none has left town since this morning, an' if she didn't have a horse to get away on before she robbed the bank, she must have got one afterward."

As they trudged southward down the alley, Hart's brow

creased in thought. Shortly before they left the alley by way of a sideroad he said, "Maybe it wasn't a woman, Whit. One of those other ones dressed like a woman. Maybe this was another one like that."

Whit did not comment. He was thinking along different lines. If the robber had indeed hired a horse earlier so as to be sure of escaping, then why hadn't the horse been tied in the alley behind the bank? If she had been clever enough to make up a believable story to get her inside the bank, she sure as hell would have been clever enough to have a horse tied out back to flee on.

"Something," Whit said to the harness maker as they turned westerly in the direction of the livery barn, "is missing from all this. We know who she is. We even know where she came from, that she was in some way joined up with those dead men, an' we know how she worked her scheme to get inside the damned bank with a concealed six-gun. Tom, we know just about everything except how she got away."

The harness maker was gazing across Main Street toward the livery barn runway, which was gloomily dark, when he replied. "Whatever is missing," he said bleakly, "isn't going to save her—even if she really is a 'she.' "

Whit did not say another word as they moved into the broad roadway on their way toward the livery barn, where someone down the runway was dragging an old wooden chair with him as he stood on it to light the overhead lamps.

The reason he did not say anything was because he was not sure that the harness maker was right.

16

A Baffling Trail

THE liveryman's name was Jake Spooner. He was a slovenly, taciturn individual who had very little faith in humanity and chewed tobacco. He listened to what Whit said, then shook his head. "After the way you fellers left some of my animals way to hell and gone over in them foothills I been real particular who I rent horses to, and none of my animals been let out today. Not to a woman, not to anyone at all. And there's somethin' else. Who's goin' to pay me for draggin' those dead horses out of the road?"

Tom Hart stared at the liveryman, looking irritated. "You'll get your horses back."

"Yeah, maybe next Christmas. Who's goin' to pay me for draggin' those—?"

"Ask Mister Flaherty," Hart said crossly. "They was his animals."

The liveryman glared at Hart but did not pursue this topic. He shifted his gaze to Whit Pierson. "A woman? A woman robbed the bank with a passel of guards inside along with Charley Bonner? That's pretty hard to believe."

Whit did not allow this subject to derail him. "She didn't leave town on a stage, Jake, and there was no sign of a horse in the alley behind the bank. That leaves your livery stock."

Spooner waved his arm. "Look for yourself. Every stall is full and out back the corrals . . . Whit, I know every head of livestock I own an' I'm here to tell you none of 'em are missing." He paused to put an unfriendly glance in Tom Hart's direction. "A woman," he said scornfully.

Hart nodded. "She's gone and so is the eight thousand dollars from the bank."

Spooner's eyes snapped wide. "Eight thousand? Hey, I had seven hunnert in my account up there."

Hart smiled. "Not anymore you don't have. Let's go, Whit."

They went up to the Waterhole Saloon. Doughbelly was doing a thriving business again. They settled in at the bar and Flaherty, sitting on Whit's left, said, "I been up to Muller's place." He shook his head. "I think your town marshal is touch and go." He turned to smile a little at them, his craggy, lined face showing no humor and plenty of malevolence. "Too bad that hefty one with the whiskers didn't make it. I'd have liked to lean on the rope that pulled him up."

Hart leaned far forward to see the speaker as he spoke to him. "What did Doc say, Mister Flaherty?"

"I just told you. Touch and go. If the bullet had hit him square in the guts he'd be dead. Seems that he was maybe a foot or two ahead of the feller with the whiskers when he got shot. The bullet went in his side and come out near his belly button. From there it must have struck the fork of Given's saddle, or maybe it missed that too." Flaherty nodded acknowledgement when Doughbelly came along, then said, "The doctor says it ain't the wound that might carry him off, because as near as he can figure, it didn't do any killin' damage inside. It's the loss of blood. A man can bleed out up to a point. Beyond that point his body can't make no new blood fast enough to keep him from dying."

Hart still leaned over the bar as he said, "Is he conscious?"

"No. Accordin' to the doctor he comes in an' fades out." Flaherty looked around at them, eyes speculative. "You find that bank-robbin' lady?"

Hart eased back off the bar as Whit replied. "No."

Flaherty thought for a moment before speaking again.

"She's out there, boys, but with night comin' she'd be harder to find than a snort in a whirlwind. Which way did her tracks go?"

They explained about that and old Flaherty slouched lower against the bar before speaking again. "Well now, losing eight thousand dollars ain't goin' to set well in Beaverton, is it?"

Whit took that personally. "I'm not the marshal. Neither is Tom."

Flaherty signaled for service, and as Doughbelly came scurrying back red-faced and sweating, the old cowman chuckled. "No, neither of you boys is, but as far as I can see you two been the only ones since this mess started that been in on it from the beginnin' and done the most. Your lawman isn't goin' to do anything for a month or two, if ever. Did you know that the gent with the thick spectacles who runs the stage outfit lost fifteen hunnert dollars to the lady bank robber?"

They hadn't known, and right now they were not very interested. Hart was tired and exasperated. Whit was also tired, but he felt like a dog with a bone: he didn't want the damned thing but he'd be damned if he'd let someone else have it.

Flaherty went on speaking in his dry, mildly sarcastic way, but he seemed to be thinking out loud rather then addressing anyone in particular. "She didn't leave on a stage. She didn't have no horse tied out in the alley behind the bank to escape on. She didn't have no wings as near as I can figure from the descriptions of her I've heard, an' I know In'ians believe folks can make themselves invisible, but I don't believe that neither. What does that leave?"

Whit motioned Doughbelly away when he arrived with a poised bottle. "It leaves something I don't like to think about."

Flaherty turned his head. "Think about it anyway."

"She's still here. She didn't leave town."

Flaherty's face broke into a smile. He thumped the bartop for service, and when Doughbelly arrived he told him to fetch a bottle and leave it. Then he leaned sideways to look at Whit and Tom. "That's what I been thinkin' since I've listened to all the talk. Now then, Mister Stage Driver, you and your partner lived in Beaverton for some time—you know just about everyone and every place. Let's take this bottle over yonder to that empty table and do some figuring." Flaherty did not wait to see if they liked his suggestion; he gripped the bottle by the neck in one hand, his sticky little glass in the other, and moved over to stake a claim on the empty table before someone else did.

The two trailed after him, dour and silent. When they were all seated, the cowman placed the bottle in the center of the table and gently removed a cigar from a shirt pocket, spat the bitten end onto the floor, lighted up amid a cloud of fragrant smoke, waved it away, and said, "Where?"

Whit felt for his cut plug and spoke while slicing off a cud with his clasp knife. "I don't know. If she's got friends here she might be anywhere, but if she's a stranger to Beaverton . . ." Whit got the chew settled against his cheek and gazed across the table. "She could be anywhere from the livery barn loft to someone's chicken shed." He chewed briefly then spoke again. "If she don't have friends in town, then she's goin' to have to get food and water, and unless she robs a house, she'll have to get the grub from the general store."

Flaherty poured their glasses full, wearing a little smile. As he leaned back he emitted small clouds of bluish smoke, like puffballs. "Unless she's already hid in the store," he said.

Whit considered the jolt glass without touching it. "Maybe. After the fight started ten people could have sneaked into Coggins's store from out back and walked off with his money drawer. He was out front with the rest of us, watching the battle."

"Does his store have a loft?" Flaherty asked.

The harness maker answered. "It's got three rooms upstairs where Walt's clerk lives."

"You boys might start with that, an' if she ain't hidin' there, you might try the livery barn. Otherwise, you can sweep the town from north to south along Main Street, and if that don't produce nothin', you can start with the houses. The storekeeper's got a two-story house. I saw him come out of it this morning real early. There are a few others with upstairs to them."

Flaherty paused to tip ash onto the floor and reach for his whiskey glass. After downing his jolt he chuckled at their faces. "Well, no one else is goin' to do it, I can tell you that from listenin' at the bar, because no one else has yet figured out that she ain't fifteen miles away on horseback an' still going."

"Maybe she is," stated the harness maker, who did not rate old Flaherty very high among his acquaintances, and also because he just naturally took the opposite view when he could. "Just because the liveryman says she didn't get a horse from him an' no stages have left town don't mean she couldn't have stolen a horse and be more'n fifteen miles away by now."

Flaherty gazed dispassionately at the bottle for a moment, then shoved away from the table and arose. "It's been a pretty wild day, gents, an' a man my age needs his repose. I'm goin' up to the rooming house. You boys be careful. If you come onto that little lady, she might just damned well blow you out of your boots."

They watched him depart. When the spindle door swung closed behind him Doughbelly came along with an outstretched hand. Hart scowled. "Didn't Flaherty pay for the bottle?"

Doughbelly wagged his head, eyed Whit in particular, and said, "Nope, an' I'll be damned if someone else didn't snooker you besides Charley."

"How much?"

Doughbelly raised the bottle, placed four fingers against it to measure how much had been taken out, put the bottle down, and said, "Six bits."

Hart reacted as though he had been stung. "Six bits! That bottle wasn't full when he brought it over here."

Doughbelly remained unperturbed in the face of the harness maker's ire. "No, it wasn't. But it was full before you boys walked in. Flaherty'd been nursin' drinks out of it for an hour."

Whit put a silver cartwheel beside the bottle on the table and sighed. He saw Sam Holt walk in and stop to peer around. Lamplight bounced off his thick glasses. Sam saw Whit and Hart, swerved in their direction as Doughbelly was departing, pulled out the chair Mike Flaherty had vacated, and said, "Charley's in bed sick."

This was not an earthshaking announcement. Whit and Tom looked stonily at the stage company owner until he removed his glasses and dug out the blue bandanna. As he was polishing the lenses he also said, "Walt's lookin' for some place to put those saddlebags with the stolen money off the stage."

Hart's brows went up a little. "What's wrong with where they are? His safe's as good as any other—"

"He told me he don't want that much money in his store, what with outlaws comin' and goin', even female ones." Sam put his glasses back on, leaned forward, and lowered his voice. "He wants me to keep it hid up at the stage company office."

Both the other men stared. Whit said, "You don't have a safe."

Sam's reply was short. "But I got a lot of hidin' places."

"Did you agree to take it?"

Sam nodded, looking from one of them to the other, and when Hart opened his mouth to protest, Whit nudged his leg under the table and smiled at Sam. "I expect you do have.

Hide it real good, Sam. Come on, Tom, let's go down to the café."

The harness maker did not open his mouth until they were outside in the settling evening, then he screwed up his face. "Why did you do that?"

Whit halted in front of the café. "I got an idea. It may not work. I'm not real hopeful about it, but it beats tryin' to search every building. Sam will hide the money, you and I'll sort of hint around town that he's got it. Then we can do a little searching at the store, the livery barn, and a few other places while we're waitin' to see if she hears where the money is and maybe tries to get it."

"Why would she do that? She's already got eight thousand dollars."

"Well, maybe she won't, but as long as she can't leave town on one of Sam's stages and can't get a horse from Spooner, and with time to set and fidget, maybe she'll get greedy. If she don't, we'll still be searchin' for her."

Hart entered the café, shaking his head. But he did not say anything until they'd had supper and were back outside. Then he said, "She's not goin' to fall for that, Whit. This here is the lady who lied her convincin' way into the bank, remember."

Whit nodded, not in agreement, but because he had thought of something else. As they crossed the road toward the leather works he said, "One of us better go tell Dough-belly to put some town possemen around tonight, to watch for someone tryin' to steal a horse out of someone's shed, or maybe from Spooner's corrals."

"He'll know she's still in town."

Whit was not concerned about that. "Everyone is goin' to figure that out for themselves by daybreak when it's clear she didn't leave any tracks. You want to go up there or shall I?"

Hart glanced in the direction of the saloon lights. "I'll go. That darned whelp, chargin' you seventy-five cents for what was drunk out of that bottle."

Whit reached the west side of the road, stepped up onto the plankwalk, and watched his friend going toward the saloon. He carved an after-supper cud and tongued it into place before turning northward in the direction of Doctor Muller's residence and, beyond that, the rooming house.

17

After Dark

DOCTOR Muller was sitting in a rocker on the front porch with a cigar and a glass of watered whiskey when Whit Pierson came through the gate. Muller waited until Whit was at the foot of the steps before offering to provide some whiskey. Whit declined, and ignoring an empty chair, leaned on the porch railing as he said, "Lots of stories goin' around about Jack."

Muller nodded wryly. "There always are—about anyone I got up here." He flicked ash. "This is good whiskey, sure you don't want a glass?"

"No, thanks. Tom, Flaherty, and I just about killed a bottle at the Waterhole a little while ago . . . How is Jack?"

The doctor removed his cigar before replying. "About this time tomorrow I can make a fair guess. If he hangs on that long, I'd say he's got a chance." He bit down on the cigar again, leaned over to get up, and spoke around the cigar. "Come on inside, I want to show you something."

They went to Muller's tidy little office, where Carl turned up a lamp and pointed to some articles on a round-topped oak table. "That came from the pockets of those three dead outlaws. I got them out back in the embalming shed." Muller moved to the oak table and picked up a limp scrap of paper and held it toward Whit Pierson. Uneven, large round scribble, of the variety a child learning to write might make, formed several words.

Whit read them aloud. "Lizzie in Tombstone next month."

Muller trickled smoke as he said, "According to what I heard that woman who robbed the bank was named Elizabeth. Would that be Lizzie?"

Whit put the paper down and ran his eyes over what else had been dumped there: several clasp knives, soiled bandannas, silver and paper money, personal odds and ends including a ball of harness thread with two snelled fishhooks imbedded in it.

"It could be the same Lizzie. Whose pocket was that paper in?"

"The heavyset man with dark whiskers. Incidentally, his name was Curt Moran." Muller pointed to what remained of someone's trouser belt. It was bullet-torn and caked with dried blood, but the name that had been carved into the back of it was legible.

"Any other names, Carl?"

"No. If you want to see the bodies we can go—"

"No thanks."

"All right. For a fact, they aren't much to look at it. It took a little time puttin' them back together."

As they walked back through to the front porch Whit had an odd thought. If Elizabeth Harding the lady bank robber was indeed the head outlaw's friend and they had meant to meet in Tombstone, sure as hell she saw her burly boyfriend and his companions get shot all to hell in the roadway yesterday, and that would have an effect on her, regardless of her other problems.

He left Doctor Muller's place and strolled thoughtfully up to the Beaverton rooming house, found Pete Gomez out back in the bathhouse making noises like a strangling whale, and spoke through the door to him.

Pete knew about the robbery. He knew how much money had been taken and that the robber had been a woman. When Whit asked if she had stayed at his rooming house, Pete replied that she had and as soon as he got his britches on he'd show Whit the room.

Whit moved away a short distance to scrutinize the heavens. It was a flawless late-springtime night with a sickle moon that gave no light, and every star was pegged into its proper place, creating an accumulation of brilliant little ice chips that did give off light. Not much, but enough for Pete and Whit to make their way to the rear of the big old ramshackle building.

The woman's room was up near the front door on the left side. As Pete was lighting a lamp he said, "She's the kind of customer I like. Even made up her bed before leaving." Pete stepped to the floor after hanging the lamp. "She tol' me her name was Elizabeth Holden."

Whit nodded. That was close and maybe it was her name. He'd have bet a new hat the first name was hers anyway. He told Pete that he thought the woman had not escaped, that she might be hiding in town. The Mexican's dark eyes widened steadily into a stare.

"After she robbed the bank?"

"Maybe. Maybe she figured we'd go rushin' off in all directions, lookin' for her, which would leave her plenty of open space to escape in after we was all gone. Maybe not. All I can tell you for a fact, Pete, is that she's as *coyote* as they come."

Pete threw his arms wide. "But here—in town?"

Whit grinned at him. "In your loft. In your cellar. Maybe even in one of your sheds out back." Whit was in the dim hallway, heading for the front door, when he said, "Keep your eyes open. Might be a good idea to go through your rooms every now and then. But be careful, she's got a double-action Colt."

On his way southward through the darkened town he was parallel to Carl Muller's picket fence when the doctor arose from his rocker and called.

"Whit, Jack's conscious. I told him what happened after the gunfight. I told him you're heading-up the hunt for the bank robber. He'd like to see you."

Whit paused in the gateway. He wasn't heading-up the hunt for the bank robber. He wasn't heading-up anything. Everyone in town was interested and involved. When he reached the porch amd mentioned these things Carl did not argue, he simply stood with a large hand gripping the doorknob while gazing impassively at Pierson. Then he opened the door and jerked his head.

There was a small lamp burning on a table near the door of Marshal Given's room. Inside, the room smelled powerfully of carbolic acid. The light was feeble, but the man lying flat out in the bed was clearly visible. He had turned his head when the door opened.

Whit was shocked at his appearance. Normally a ruddy, robust-looking individual, Given looked now as though each breath could be his last one. His coloring was putty gray, his eyes were shadowed by dark rings, and they were sunken. He had no expression, his features had the identical look of total detachment dead people showed.

Doctor Muller went to the bedside and leaned, feeling for a pulse. When the lawman's eyes moved wearily to his face Muller said, "Better, Jack. Still weak but steadier now . . . Whit Pierson is here."

Muller stepped aside. Whit moved close and smiled gently as Given spoke with a sluggish drag to his voice. "Good thing you didn't ride gun-guard with me, Whit."

"I guess so. Maybe you hadn't ought to be talking, Jack."

Given ignored that. "There's a woman, Whit. The hefty one named Moran told me about her."

Whit nodded. "Yeah. We know. She robbed the bank yesterday before the shootin' started. Made off with eight thousand dollars. We can't find her, Jack."

Given's eyes drifted over to Doctor Muller, who spread his hands. "You didn't stay conscious long enough for me to tell you."

Whit caught the lawman's attention again. "It don't seem that she left town. We got possemen lookin' for her."

Given spoke again in a fading tone. "She's Moran's sweetheart. She's the one who told them that money was comin' south on your stage . . ."

"Yeah. We know that, Jack."

"An' they're goin' to meet in Tombstone, get married, and go down over the line into Messico. Moran told me that."

Whit nodded again.

Given seemed to be trying to rally his strength. "Notify the law down in Tombstone. Tell them they're coming. Tell 'em why we want them."

Doctor Muller moved closer. "That's enough," he told the wounded man. "Whit'll look after things. Get some sleep, Jack. I'll look in on you later." Muller jerked his head and led the way back to the front porch, where he wagged his head. "That's bad for him."

Whit said nothing because there was nothing to be said.

Doctor Muller gazed out into the darkened roadway. He remained silent for so long Whit thought he might have forgotten he was not alone. Then Muller turned back to him. "I have a bad feeling, Whit. I've handled many like that— they make one last rally to get something off their chests, then . . ."

Whit stepped to the edge of the porch. "Good night, Carl."

As he trudged southward he thought bitterly that there was not going to be any marriage in Arizona and no flight over the border down into Mexico, and if he could possibly prevent it, no one was going to leave Beaverton who had been involved in the bank robbery.

Sam Holt was leaving the corralyard as Whit came along. He had to wait until they were close enough to touch before he knew who it was. Holt's limited visibility became even more limited after sundown. He spoke from the gateway shadows. "We snuck those saddlebags over here in the dark. I hid them where nobody'll ever find them. Are you heading for the saloon?"

Whit had been heading for his house out behind the

smithy, but he could use a drink, so he nodded. As they crossed the road Sam spoke again. "Too bad about Jack. I didn't think he'd make it anyway."

Whit stopped in the center of the road. "What the hell are you talking about?"

"He died a couple hours back."

"Did he? I just came from talkin' to him."

Sam was rattled. He was also apologetic when he sensed the anger of his former employee. "That's what I heard. That he died."

"You ought to know better than to believe town gossip, Sam. And don't start wipin' your damned glasses." Whit stamped away without looking to see if he still had a companion. He didn't.

The stage-company owner remained in place until a pair of riders had to cut out around him, then he too struck out for the Waterhole Saloon, but when he was inside he avoided the vacant place farther down the counter where Whit was watching Doughbelly fill a jolt glass.

Old Flaherty, farther up the bar, took his glass with him and went down to stake out a piece of the counter beside Pierson. Whit put a sour look upon the old cowman, downed his drink, and counted out several silver coins, which he placed inside the empty glass, then turned and walked back out into the warm night.

Across the road there was a light burning at the harness works. He went over there, had to rattle the door because Tom had locked up. When Tom opened the door, wearing a scowl, Whit shouldered past and went to stand with his back to the iron stove. He was still irritated.

Hart's scowl vanished as he studied his friend's face. Without speaking he went around behind his counter, groped for his whiskey bottle, and set it atop the counter as he said, "You get dog bit?"

"No. I just heard that Jack had died, and hell's bells, I had just come from talkin' to him."

"Who said he'd died?"

"Sam Holt."

Tom took a long pull from the bottle, wiped his mouth on a limp sleeve, and blew out a flammable breath. "That shouldn't upset you, for crissake. You worked for Sam for years. You know that if he had a brain he'd take it out an' play with it." Tom pushed the bottle to the edge of his counter, but his guest ignored it, so Tom said, "Well, they took the money bags over to him, and I whispered this secret to some fellers who came in here before suppertime. Later, when I was over at the saloon, I confided in a couple of other fellers. One of 'em was Buffler Stoneman. He liked to chewed me up one side an' down the other for lettin' on about somethin' he said was supposed to be a secret."

Whit roused himself. "What about the possemen?"

"Doughbelly set them to patrolling. One of 'em was the feller that lady hit up alongside the head. I wouldn't want to be in her boots if he catches her."

"And Spooner?"

Tom grimaced. "He's like old Flaherty, makes it real hard for a man to like him. He told me him an' one of his hostlers is goin' to spend the night in the barn with guns in their laps, an' I wouldn't put it past Spooner to shoot a woman."

Whit relented, took a swallow of Tom's whiskey, and made a horrible face. "Is that some of Doughbelly's dregs?"

Tom straightened up. "Dregs! I'll have you know I bought two bottles of that liquor off a trader last spring. You can see right there on the label it was bottled in bond."

Whit was struggling for breath when he replied. "From a trader, an' you took his word?"

"It don't bother me an' I been nippin' on it all summer. You got weak guts, Whit, that's what's wrong with you." Tom snatched the bottle and put it out of his friend's reach.

When Whit had caught his breath and had mopped his eyes, he leaned on the bar, sucking air for a moment before speaking again. "Where is she, Tom? Did Sam set someone to watching his office and corralyard tonight?"

Hart did not have answers to either of those questions. "All I know is that it's all over town that she's most likely hidin' out right here under our noses. I'd say the odds of her not gettin' caught are maybe five hunnert to one. As for Sam and his damned hidey-hole, I got no idea where it is an' don't care—I just want her to come sneakin' out of cover. At the corralyard, down at the livery barn, even among the horse sheds behind town." Hart changed the subject. "When you was up yonder did Carl mention visiting Charley?"

"No."

"Well, he got taken to his bed about an hour or so after the robbery. His wife told me over at the store, where she was loadin' up on bottles of Doctor Bosworth's Wonder Worker Remedy, that he don't even eat, just lies there sweatin' and groanin'."

Whit was rummaging for his molasses-cured when he said, "Too bad. That lady bank robber upset everyone. By the way, that hefty feller with the whiskers who shot Jack—his name was Curt Moran and he and the lady outlaw was supposed to meet down at Tombstone and get married next month."

The harness maker stared. "Where'd you find that out?"

"From our 'dead' town marshal up at Carl's place. Moran told him that, an' it seemed to be the truth. There was a little note among the things from Moran's pocket mentioning it."

Tom leaned down on his scarred counter, gazing thoughtfully in the direction of the iron stove. "And she knows Moran is dead. She was still in town when I shot him off his horse north of town. Maybe she was beneath me'n Pete in her room. Wherever she was, she sure as hell knows her sweetheart is dead. So she won't be going to Tombstone, will she?"

"No. Not if that was her only reason for going. An' not if I can help it."

Hart straightened up, put his bottle below the counter,

and said, "Whit, she'd be in pretty bad shape, wouldn't you say? It comes to me that all she'll want right now is to get the hell as far away from Beaverton as she can get . . . She's not goin' to try for that money hid out at the corralyard, she's going to get the hell away from here."

Whit hid a yawn behind an upraised hand before replying. "Maybe. Seems likely." He walked as far as the door before saying the rest of it. "If there are possemen watching tonight, she's goin' to have to be awful lucky. The only way she's goin' to escape is with a horse. On top of one or behind one. She can't do it on foot. She can try doin' it that way, but my guess is that she's too smart to attempt it. Good night, Tom. See you in the morning."

After Whit left the harness shop he crossed the road and barely even nodded when he passed other pedestrians, most of whom were armed men trying to seem casual as they strolled through town.

By the time he got down to his house behind the smithy he was ready to go to sleep standing up. He did not even light a lamp as he got ready to bed down.

The last thing he did was drape the shellbelt with its holstered Colt over the back of the chair at his bedside, where he also put his shirt and britches, with the hat on top.

18

About Midnight

EVEN in crisis, Beaverton was typical of frontier towns; excepting Saturday nights, people retired two or three hours after sundown. Doughbelly closed the Waterhole about ten o'clock, doused the lights, and retired to his room out back. A few lights glowed here and there through town, but about the only ones that burned all night were the pair of carriage lamps on each side of Spooner's doorless wide opening to his barn, and two more similar lights up at the corralyard. By dawn their bowls were usually empty.

This particular night the pattern of retiring early prevailed, although by now everyone knew the bank robber was likely still in town. A few bleak souls sat up with their livestock in little sheds or barns around town, armed to the gills. Six or eight town possemen took stationary positions in places that seemed to them to be adequately strategic. Sam Holt had promised extra pay to some corralyard men for standing guard all night; they hid around the yard with guns, struggling to remain awake as the night wore along.

The town was quiet until about eleven o'clock, when a dog on the east side began caterwauling, probably over the scent of nocturnal prowlers such as the foraging raccoons that made routine raids along alleyways where refuse bins stood. This racket was taken up by other town dogs, most of whom had not detected varmit scent but who appeared to feel honor bound to join in the bedlam.

Occasionally a dog would let out a high sharp yelp, audible

above the more menacing sounds, when some irate sleeper hurled something, but most sleepers were not disturbed. They had become inured to this sort of racket.

Whit Pierson was. It helped too that his little house out behind the blacksmith's shop was at the extreme lower end of town and the barking was more northerly, up where residences were not only a little more pretentious but also closer to one another.

Whit's profession was a routine of scrambled schedules. Because of this he had become conditioned to sleeping like a log when the opportunity to sleep arrived. Also, over the past few days he had missed a lot of sleep, and sleep was a cumulative thing. A man could go for several days without it, but when he finally bedded down nothing short of a cannonade or a violent earthquake was likely to awaken him.

Snakes excepted.

The alarm was a silent scream in his subconscious mind before he opened both eyes in total darkness, holding himself motionless, scarcely breathing as a cold, slithering object crossed his throat from right to left with infinite slowness.

The drowsiness that commonly lingered briefly after someone awakens lasted no more than a couple of seconds, hastened in its departure by Whit Pierson's lifelong aversion to snakes.

He stared straight upward where the wooden ceiling was dimly visible by weak starshine coming through his only bedroom window.

The snake's clammy underside finally trailed off to the left. Whit did not move for what he thought would be enough time for the creature to be unable to coil when he moved, then he jackknifed into a sitting position, rolling his blankets to the left with one hand while using the other hand to lever himself in the opposite direction where his shellbelt was draped from the chair.

As his feet hit the floor, one hand found the shellbelt in

darkness, scrambled down it to the holster—and there was no gun.

His heart was pounding. He leaned to feel elsewhere for the weapon, abandoned the search, got to his feet mindful of the saying that snakes traveled in pairs, and took one long step toward the wall bench, struck a match, lighted the coal-oil lamp, and swung it as he searched the area around his naked feet for a reptile.

A pale ghost standing in a corner moved slightly and caught his attention. He could make out the silhouette fairly well, but the cocked pistol pointing squarely at his chest was clearer because lamplight reflected off it. It was a six-gun, smaller than the regulation kinds, and it had a very short barrel.

He stood in his underwear without moving as his eyes traveled from the pointed gun to the shadowy face above and behind it. His breath hissed out. For a long moment he and the woman with dark curly hair looked straight at each other, then Whit's heartbeat slackened back down to normal. He said, "For crissake, lady, all you had to do was shake me awake." He turned his head along with the lamp, looking for the snake.

She did not lower the gun nor ease the hammer down. "I thought pulling that wet rag over your neck would be better. You'd be less likely to yell or lash out."

He ignored the weapon, put his lamp on the wall bench, and went to sit on the edge of the bed, looking at her. She watched him, tracking every movement with the cocked gun; he finally slapped his upper legs with both hands and said, "Sit down. If you fire that gun, half the possemen patrolling town will be down here before you can get out of here."

She sat on the bench near the little lamp but did not lower the gun. She said, "If I shoot this gun, cowboy, you'll never know whether anyone came or not."

He looked down and reached swiftly for his trousers, which he placed across his lap. The woman's dark eyes and delicate features were like stone. Whit corrected her, "I'm not a cowboy, I'm a stage driver."

Her dark eyes turned speculative. "A stage driver?" She finally lowered the gun but did not ease off the hammer. "You drive stages out of Beaverton?"

He let go a rattling breath, the last vestige of his earlier fright. She was young, in her early twenties but maybe younger. She was very pretty even in poor light, or possibly because of poor light. As he studied her, he thought of the men she had struck in the face up at the bank, but when next he spoke it was in response to her question about his trade as a stage driver.

"Well, I drove for the local stage outfit until I quit a while back. You know why I quit? Because I was herding the coach that brought that three thousand dollars down from Meadowville, an' they hadn't told me I'd be hauling bullion nor put a gun-guard aboard with me. And if your friends had taken your advice about stoppin' the coach in the middle of nowhere to rob it, right now I most likely wouldn't be sitting here breathin' in and out." He glared at her. "An' if you think I'm goin' to help you get out of here you're wrong. Anyway, I don't drive for the company anymore, so I wouldn't be able to sneak you aboard a stage."

She had been gazing steadily at him through his statement, with the gun pointing floorward but still cocked. She did not seem ready to speak, so he also said, "How did you get in here?"

She jutted her chin. "That little window. It wasn't latched." As she faced him again she said, "It was the farthest house from the middle of town where all the commotion was. It's out behind the shoeing works, pretty much away from everyone else, and it was at the lower end of town across the road from all those livery horses."

He reached for his shirt and as he was shrugging into it, he said, "They'd kill you over there, lady. Every place in town we figured you might try to get an animal has armed men waiting in hiding." He buttoned the shirt and started to lift his britches. She was staring at him. He left the trousers in his lap as he said, "Turn your head."

She did not move. He cleared his throat, met her dark gaze, and reddened in the gloom. "Lady, you got the gun. You emptied my holster. I got to put my pants on. You like to scairt me to death with the goddamned snake trick, the least you can do is let me stand up and get my britches on."

She turned her head sideways, where she could still watch him with one eye, and because he knew that was the best he was going to get, he stood up and yanked on his britches as rapidly as possible. He turned his back to her while buttoning them, then dropped back down on the edge of the bed, breathing a little faster. She straightened forward, as expressionless as before. Just for a very brief moment he felt sorry for her, then he remembered that posseman with the blood-clotted hair up at the bank and leaned to pull on his boots. As he leaned, he saw his six-gun. It had been placed on the floor and shoved with a toe under the bed. He sat up again, thinking the damned gun might as well be on the moon. She was about ten feet from him with her cocked Colt Lightning.

He was looking at her when she quietly spoke. "What happened to those three riders who got shot in the roadway?"

"That's what happened to them—they got shot. They rode into an ambush."

"How did you know they were coming?"

"We trailed them into the mountains, snuck close, and heard that heavyset one named Moran talkin' about comin' back here to bust the bank because they didn't believe anyone in town would expect them to do that. We hurried back to get here ahead of them and set up the ambush. Lady, I'm sorry about Moran. I'm maybe the only one in town who is, because he shot our town marshal who may very well die from the wound." Whit was gaining confidence. "We know you and Moran was to meet down in Arizona, get married, and go down into Mexico. Marshal Given told us Moran told him that, and there was a piece of paper in Moran's pocket about it."

"Why would Curt tell your town marshal?"

"Because they took our town marshal captive and kept him with them right up until they rode into town. Lady, I'll answer all your questions if you will answer just one for me. Why did you come down here to rob our bank?"

She looked at the gun in her lap, slowly eased down the hammer, then raised the barrel with her thumb on the hammer and pointed it across at Pierson. "After they left, I thought they would do as I had said, stop the stage somewhere, rob it, and head for Arizona. I waited several days before quitting the bank up in Meadowville to take a stage down their back-trail. I had to know if they had been successful. I didn't really come down here to rob the Beaverton bank."

"Lady, you had a leather money pouch," said Whit. She nodded about that. "They're large enough for what a person needs while traveling. I'd used one of them before. I used one this time. So did other people who worked at the Meadowville bank." She looked over at him. "I didn't bring it with me because I planned to rob your bank, but when I got down here and heard what had happened, and that Curt, along with Jim and Fred, was riding into an ambush, I decided to raid the bank first, then steal a horse and race out there to stop them before they reached town, and leave the territory with them."

Whit scratched his head, gazed around the room, which was turning chilly, and said, "I need some coffee. How about you?"

She nodded.

He regarded her thoughtfully. "Are you hungry?"

"Yes."

"You goin' to shoot me if I go out into the kitchen?"

"I'm going to come with you."

She trailed him, still pointing the gun at him. When he lighted a larger lamp and went to sift in the firebox for coals, of which there were none, he went to the kindling box as he said, "If you hadn't hit those fellers in the bank . . ." He was arranging paper beneath the kindling when she replied.

"I wouldn't have hit that young one if he hadn't laughed at me and tried to knock my gun aside. The older man, the one the others called Charley, refused to open the safe. I didn't have time for arguing. I didn't hit him very hard. He fell down, but when he recovered he opened the safe. I think he was dazed."

Whit said, "Yeah, he was," closed the firebox door, and went to a window to knock the stale grounds from his speckleware coffeepot. He filled it with water from the sink-bucket on his way back to the stove and dropped in a couple of fistfulls of ground beans. "Where is the money, Lizzie?"

"Where you won't find it."

He became busy with an old iron skillet, some eggs, and a bowl of flour, baking powder, and water from which he made biscuits a man could have rolled from Beaverton all the way down to Livermore without cracking.

He was silent during long moments of thought. When she moved closer, where he had placed a tin cup after indifferently rinsing it in the same sink-bucket he'd got the coffee water from, he gazed speculatively at her. "I got an idea," he said, and poured two tin cups full of coffee strong enough to float horseshoes. She picked up one of the cups and stepped away. "Give them back the money, Lizzie, and—"

"They shot Curt. What I should have done was ride straight down through town with a gun in each hand."

He held his tin cup chest-high, looking at her. She jutted her chin. "Don't burn the eggs."

She went to a little stool to watch and sip the coffee. When he was putting food onto a pair of thick crockery plates she said, "What is your name?"

"Whitney Pierson. Folks call me Whit."

"You'd better get married before too long, Whit. If you always eat like this you aren't going to have any stomach left."

He put the plates on his handmade little kitchen table, waited until she was seated before shoving toward her the water glass that held knives, forks, and spoons, and scowled at her. "Are you goin' to eat one-handed?"

She selected a fork and knife from the tumbler while nodding her head. "Yes. The gun is pointed at your middle from beneath the table."

He watched her eat. She appeared half-starved. Once more he felt sorry for her. "Lizzie, listen to me—"

"It's the other way around. *You* listen to *me*. You are going to help me leave Beaverton."

"All right. You leave the eight thousand dollars behind and I'll do it."

She looked steadily at him. The only sound in the little room was made by oily steel rubbing over oily steel as she cocked the gun under the table.

He went to work on his eggs and biscuits, which he habitually washed down with strong coffee. "You'll never make it alone."

"I won't have to, Mister Pierson. Do you have next of kin?"

He chewed, swallowed, reached for the coffee cup, and would not look at her.

19

Too Late

IT was early morning, the moon was gone and starshine lingered in a diminished capacity. He cleaned up after their meal while she perched on the stool and watched everything he did. When he turned to ask sarcastically about the cast on her arm she snapped at him.

"Never mind, just figure out how you are going to get me away from here."

He draped his flour-sack dish towel before turning around. "Don't saddle me with your troubles, lady."

She smiled sweetly. "That would be better than burying you with them, wouldn't it?"

He snorted at her. "You're not going to use that gun."

"If I can't get away, then they will catch me anyway, won't they? So what would I have to lose?"

He leaned toward the window to scan the heavens. It was still dark out, intensely so, which meant that dawn was on the way. He turned back. "You figure things pretty good for a woman."

She did not respond.

"The money don't belong to you. The only reason you stole it was to prove something. I don't know what an' I don't care. But I'm not goin' to help you unless you tell me where the money is."

The little gun tipped upward in the direction of his chest.

He eyed it dispassionately, turned to look out the window again, and spoke while his back was to her. "It's not goin' to

146

stay dark much longer, Lizzie. After daylight comes, a troop of cavalry couldn't smuggle you out of Beaverton." He faced her again, this time with thick arms crossed over his chest. He grinned a little. "Mexican standoff. Go ahead an' shoot."

For a full twenty seconds neither of them moved, spoke, or took his eyes off the other. "You murdered him," she half whispered.

"I didn't murder anyone," he replied quietly. "I didn't even draw a gun or get off a shot. Things were happening everywhere. It was all I could do to just keep track and watch."

"You know what I meant. The town murdered him."

He let go with a long breath. "He rode into an ambush, an' if he hadn't been crazy enough to come back here, he'd still be alive. What was the town supposed to do—let him ride in, usin' our lawman as a shield, rob the bank, most likely kill the lawman, then ride out? Lizzie . . . I shouldn't say this, but he was a fool."

Her hand whitened from gripping the Colt Lightning. He saw that and briefly hung fire, suspecting he might have gone too far.

"From today onward," he said, "this is your world an' your life. Not his. I'm sorry if you loved him, but it would have happened like this somewhere, sometime. He's gone. You are still alive an' with a little help from me, you're goin' to be alive a long time."

Her face was wiped clear of expression, but her very dark eyes were enormous as she looked at him, until they wavered. She forced bitterness when she spoke. "You missed your trade, Whit. You should have been a preacher."

He smiled crookedly. "Strange you should say that. My grandmother wanted me to be a priest. Hell, if I'd listened to her, by now I'd be settin' in some nice cool mission somewhere drinkin' old wine, prayin', and scratchin'. Care for some more coffee?"

She made no attempt to stifle the shudder when she answered, "No."

"Well, next time you make it. I never claimed to be a cook."

She frowned faintly. "Where is the three thousand dollars they got?"

"I don't know. Hidden somewhere in town. But you better forget about that. Lizzie, it's not goin' to stay dark much longer."

She dropped her head and studied the Lightning Colt, then straightened back, and pushed it into a pocket. She looked up again. "Can you do it?"

"Get you out of here? I don't know. But I'd stand a better chance of doin' it than you'd have. Do we have a trade?"

Their eyes locked in silent combat. She said, "Eight thousand dollars is an awfully high price to pay."

"Naw it isn't. Look at me, Lizzie . . . *Goddamnit, I said look at me!* That's better. You've lost the money anyway. If they catch you, they'll get it. If I help you escape, I get it and give it back to them, but if I can sneak you away at least you won't end up in a prison. Lizzie, you're young. Likely you'll live maybe another forty years. Spread eight thousand dollars over that length of time and gettin' away free won't be much of a price to pay will it?"

She considered the earnestness of his expression, put her head slightly to one side, and said, "I hid in a hay shed near the upper end of town, then sneaked down here in darkness, and damned if I didn't have to pick a place I figured was isolated enough to be safe and have to belong to a corralyard zealot."

He laughed. "Lizzie . . . ?"

"What?"

"The money?"

"All right."

"And something else."

"What?"

"You are very pretty."

She stood away from the kitchen stool with her hand in the gun pocket. She became all-business. "How do you expect to do it—get me away from here I mean?"

He was still leaning at the sink, arms crossed. "First, let's go dig up the money."

"Would you double-cross me, Whit?"

"No, ma'am. I wouldn't double-cross you even if I had a gun an' you didn't."

She gestured. "Turn your back. Look out the window and keep looking out there until I tell you not to. *Turn!*"

He faced the wall, and while eyeing some randomly cast high stars he said, "You got it under your clothes? I don't believe it, Lizzie. There weren't no bulges."

"Just shut up and keep looking out that window!"

He leaned to see more nearly overhead where other star clusters shone softly. "Good thing for you it was paper instead of gold and silver."

There was no response, but there was a slight sound of rustling cloth.

"Lizzie, you got kinfolk?"

"Why do you want to know?"

"Well, because I'm interested is why."

"Mind your own business."

"Can I turn now?"

"If you do, I'll shoot you!"

He narrowed his eyes toward the east. There seemed to be a faint hint of pencil-thin light separating heaven from earth. "If you don't hurry up," he told her, "you are goin' to have to hide in my house all day an' wait for night to return."

Her reply was crisp. "Turn." When he did so she pointed rigidly toward the tabletop. "There is your damned eight thousand dollars."

"Are you sure it's all there?"

The raised arm returned to her side as she glared at him. "No, I spent some in that cow shed, living it up. The chickens and I got drunk an' danced a fandango. Of course it's all there. There wasn't any way for it not to be. I suppose you want to count it."

He raised his eyes to her face. "You have one hell of a time bein' pleasant don't you? No, I don't want to count it." His eyes raked her up and down. "You don't look any different. Well, maybe a might scrawnier around the middle."

She stood stiffly, regarding him. "I'm waiting. Like you said, we don't have much time."

He deliberately added to her irritation by slowly and methodically stacking the loose greenbacks, then hunting for something to tie them with, and the last thing he did was jerk his head for her to follow. They returned to the disheveled bedroom, and he got down on his knees, feeling for the commode pot. He placed the money in there, shoved the pot back under the bed, and stood up. "I wouldn't look in there, would you?"

She glared in silence.

He rubbed a stubbly jaw, moved to the window for another look at the sky, then faced around and eyed her briefly before going to some wall pegs where his extra clothing hung. He tossed a faded shirt onto the bed, selected a pair of trousers in no better shape, and said, "Put them on while I'm gone."

"Gone where?" She asked quickly.

"To sniff around outside. If I owned a horse it'd be easier. Since I don't, why then I got to figure a way to steal one for you. Put those things on. I'll be back in a little while."

She seemed about to speak. He ignored that and strode back to the kitchen, where he could let himself out of the house without being seen.

It was cold.

Moving quietly along the side of his house in the direction of the shoeing shop he strained for sounds. All he heard was the door of an outhouse slam up north somewhere, then a dog bark once and yip when something was thrown at it.

He crossed open space to the smithy, waited before moving

again, and worked his way into layers of sooty darkness until he could see the lighted livery barn runway across the road.

Some other time, under different circumstances, he would have willingly wagered good money that if Jake Spooner was over there, he would be sound asleep. But not tonight.

Up near Coggins's store in the middle of town a night bird called. Whit looked pained. A schoolboy could have made a better imitation.

An answering night-bird call came from the opposite side of the road in the vicinity of Carl Muller's house.

Whit moved up to the southwest corner of the shoeing shed, concealed by darkness, and squatted to watch Spooner's runway. The hanging lanterns had smoky mantles, perhaps because no one had trimmed the wicks in a while, but whatever the cause, there was only about half as much light as there should have been.

Occasionally a horse stamped or snorted, otherwise there was a depth of stillness and silence.

Whit dug out his plug, gnawed off a piece, spat, and continued to look across the road. He leaned out to look northward. At the upper end of Main Street two lanterns burned, one on each side of Sam Holt's corralyard gate. Their mantles were just as sooty as the ones in front of Spooner's barn.

Sam had about fifteen horses up there, some stalled, mostly corralled, and although his horses were large, not necessarily built for speed, they would be ridable because that was one of Sam's quirks: he would not buy a harness animal that was not also broke to ride.

But a lumpy shape appeared up in the gateway, cradling what looked at that distance and in the poor light to be a long-barreled rifle. Whit spat again. He had considered a horse from the corralyard only as an alternative to one from across the road, but that lumpy shape up yonder of a man bundled against pre-dawn chill discouraged him. The corralyard had a semicircular palisade of cedar logs, with only a little postern alley-gate in back and the much wider Main Street gate in front. If someone got cornered up there, trying to steal a horse, he couldn't get back out unless the sentinels up there were dead to the world—and obviously at least one of them wasn't.

He returned his attention to the runway, chill seeping into his marrow. The sky was beginning to get gray, and across the road a carbine-carrying, bareheaded man in bedraggled, ill-fitting clothes came out, yawned, spat, and looked up and down the road. Then he stepped to the shadowed north side of the building, leaned his Winchester aside, inched up even closer, and stood with feet spread apart looking down.

Whit raised his head to sniff the air. A faint scent of cook-stove smoke reached him. He could not see lights behind the stores lining Main Street, but he knew people were stirring, firing up for breakfast, scrubbing up by lamplight, shaving, stamping into their boots, and snapping suspenders as they adjusted their britches.

He lingered until the man alongside the barn came back around in front, carelessly carrying his Winchester. He stopped once, facing the runway, to hoist one foot and vigorously shake it, then went back down into the barn, where Spooner emerged from a small, lighted combination harness room and office to say something. The liveryman had a shellbelt around his middle with a heavy revolver pulling his trousers down on the right side.

Whit shook his head without being conscious of it. If Jake Spooner didn't look like someone's drawing of what a man wearing a weapon shouldn't look like, Whit could not imagine who would.

But a light coming grudgingly into view through the northward café window settled what Jake Spooner's ludicrous silhouette had suggested: It was too late.

Whit spat out his chew, thought a little about what now had to be done, and turned back toward his house, feeling very uncomfortable.

When he walked in the kitchen was warm and fragrant. There was a clean coffeepot on the stove and fresh water in the sink bucket, which meant she'd left the house to fill it.

He squinted against the light, shielded his eyes with a hand, and said, "Too late. The town's coming awake. Anyway, the sky is brightening."

She looked at him from near the stove. "Yes. I noticed the sky was brightening when I went out to the well."

"An' suppose someone had seen you?"

"They didn't. I was careful." She filled a tin cup and handed it to him. "You were right."

He sniffed the coffee. "About what?"

"We'll have to wait until tonight. I'll have to hide in your house all day."

He took the cup to the table, sat down, and sipped. At his surprised look, she said, "It always tastes better if you scrub out the pot now and then. Were the armed men still around?"

"Yes."

"Would you like some eggs and meat, and some decent biscuits?"

He looked up at her and smiled. "You look like a wizened tramp in those clothes."

She shot her answer right back. "Then imagine what you must look like in them."

His smile winked out. "Stick your tongue out, Lizzie."

"What for?"

"So I can see if you got a forked tongue like a snake."

She turned abruptly back to the stove.

20
Smoke

WHEN Whit entered the saddle and harness works Tom Hart was drawing his first cup of black java of the day. He nodded and gestured toward the coffeepot on the stove as he moved around to his working area and said, "Charley was in here ten minutes ago."

"I thought he was sick in bed."

"He was. Doc called it depression and told him to eat a steak, drink some whiskey, and take a hot bath. Well, he still looks like a man who's been yanked through a knothole, but at least he's back on his feet." Hart paused to swallow coffee before tying on his wax-stiff apron. "How long can a man feel sorry for himself? Anyway, it was money—his damned house didn't burn down, an' that young whippersnapper who clerks for him didn't run off in the night with his wife." Hart eyed the side of leather on his cutting table, resolutely turned his back on it, and eyed his friend. "Doughbelly told Charley that every time a dog barked last night the town possemen came a-running." He smiled maliciously. "Nothing. Some varmints in trash cans an' a horse fight. Whit, I'll lay you ten to one she's gone. Upped and disappeared."

Whit filled a greasy cup from the stove pot. "Maybe," he said, and, without thinking, raised the cup and swallowed. He put the cup aside half-empty and made a face, which the harness maker saw and glared about. "I'll never give you another cup of coffee as long as I live," he exclaimed, red in the face.

154

Whit could have replied to that too, but he didn't. He said, "Lately I been developing a nervous belly when I drink coffee," and watched the angry look fade slightly.

Mike Flaherty entered the shop, nodded on his way to the counter, and tipped back his hat as he got comfortable. "It's time for me to go home," he said, eyeing the harness maker's layout on the cutting table. "If she ain't turned up by now, she's not goin' to. I'd like to know how the hell she worked it, escapin' like she did."

As he straightened up, Flaherty also said, "Just had breakfast with the doctor. He told me Marshal Given didn't take off last night, when he should have. He said when he went in to feed him whiskeyed water this morning, the marshal had some color an' his eyes was bright." Flaherty looked pointedly at Whit Pierson. "But he's not goin' to be up and around for a spell, and you folks here in Beaverton need a lawman. Someone who'll do the job until Given's able to take over again. An' whoever fills in had ought to get a whole herd of wanted dodgers made up and mailed all over the country for that darned female outlaw."

Flaherty turned his attention to the harness maker. "I don't expect the town'll pay for my dead horses."

Hart scowled. "Why should we pay? Take it out of whatever the outlaws had, maybe auction off their saddles and spurs and all."

Flaherty shook his head at Hart. "I already looked at their outfits. Everythin' they owned, includin' the weapons, wouldn't pay for the horses. By the way, I'll keep the liveryman's animals until someone comes for them. No charge. Say, if you boys or Doughbelly are ever down my way again, stop in for a spell."

After Flaherty departed Whit said, "He's a rough old goat, but he did well by us. I like him."

Tom Hart was unwilling to go that far. "Cranky old bastard," he grumbled, but added, "well, yes, he done well by us."

The blacksmith came in carrying a torn set of leather shoeing harness. As he tossed it onto the counter he said, "Double-stitched back leather, an' look at it."

Hart and Whit looked. Hart said, "How big was the horse that busted it, Wes?"

"One of Sam's combination horses. Twelve hunnert pounds or so."

Hart handled the leather, studying his torn stitches. Eventually he said, "All right. I told you it was guaranteed, so I'll fix it without no charge. But I'm goin' to reinforce it until an elephant couldn't do that to it."

The blacksmith looked pleased, at least as pleased as it was possible for him ever to look. He turned toward Whit. "You must have cooked breakfast with pitch wood this morning. There's still black smoke comin' out of your stovepipe. My hired man wanted us to go over there just in case."

Whit felt his face losing color. "Yeah. Pitch wood. I'd better go down and—"

The blacksmith wasn't finished. "I'm surprised at you, Whit. Only greenhorns can't tell pitch wood from decent stuff."

Whit started for the door as he replied to the blacksmith. "I just shoved in a few sticks of it for kindling. Thanks, Wes, I'll go take care of it."

After Whit had fled, the blacksmith shook his head in disgust. "There are enough flue fires in town every year without someone who knows better invitin' one . . . Tom, anything new about the bank robber?"

Hart was still fingering the torn kicking-harness when he replied. "No. I was tellin' Whit, sure as hell she's gone by now."

"How?"

Hart put the leather down and scowled. "I got no idea, Wes. It's just somethin' I feel in my bones."

That annoyed the blacksmith. "With half the possemen slippin' around town all night? What's the good of havin' them if they can't even catch a woman Doc said was no bigger'n a pint of beer?"

Hart took the broken straps to his cutting table and did not look around until Wes was no longer in the shop, then he leaned on the table, glaring at the torn straps. "Twelve hunnert pound horse! I'll bet that cranky old toad went and used them straps to haul back at least two horses onto a tongue."

Walt Coggins went past, chewing a cigar; he waved casually and cut diagonally across the road in the direction of his store. Buffler Stoneman poked his head in and said, "Are you part of the town council by any chance?"

Hart shook his head. "Not this year."

"How about the storekeeper?"

"Yeah, he is, so is the banker and that old man who runs the abstract office, Mister Leathergood."

Stoneman said, "Much obliged," and straightened back. But a moment later he poked his head back in and said, "You think it'd be all right if I put in for the town marshal's job until Given can take up the slack?"

Hart was only mildly surprised. "Yeah, I guess so. Someone had better do it. Yes—go ahead and talk to Walt about it."

Tom was drawn to his doorway by the sound of Doughbelly arguing loudly with someone across the road. The man in front of the saloonkeeper was an unshorn, unwashed, faded and patched rangeman whose head-hung horse languished at the saloon tie-rack. The cowboy was unsteady on his feet, and it wasn't even ten o'clock in the morning. He also had his right hand resting on the saw-handle grips of an old six-gun in a tied-down holster.

Doughbelly was red as a beet and angry. Tom Hart saw all he had to see. He stepped back inside, got his Winchester, and returned to the doorway as the cowboy snarled and swung a roundhouse blow that missed Doughbelly by a foot. Doughbelly—shorter, thicker, and above all, stone sober—swung a short blow that caught the cowboy on the cheek and knocked him off the plankwalk against a tie-rack post. Hart moved out in front of his shop as the cowboy rolled awkwardly, got to his knees, and started to draw. Hart bellowed at him. "I'll blow your goddamn head off!"

The cowboy got to his feet and leaned on the tie-rack with his back to Doughbelly, looking straight down the barrel of Hart's Winchester. He did not say a word, but spat, hitched at his britches, went to free his horse, swung up, and put his back to everyone who was watching as he rode at a slow walk northward out of town.

Doughbelly waved at Tom and went back inside the saloon. Hart grounded his Winchester, looked southward, saw oily black smoke rising fitfully from Whit's house behind the blacksmith's shop, and went back to his cutting table.

The oily smoke was dwindling, not because anyone had done anything to dampen it, because there was very little that could be done to a stove with pitch wood inside it except wait for it to burn out, but there was a lot less smoke now than there had been when Wes had scolded Whit Pierson about using pitch wood.

The blacksmith was not the only person whose reaction to that oily black smoke rising from the Pierson stovepipe prompted irate disapproval. Whit waved his arms in the direction of the cooling stove as he said, "What in the hell are you tryin' to do, get the whole blessed town an' the fire company's water wagon down here? There's black smoke risin' above the house like an In'ian smoke signal!"

Lizzie drew herself up to appear as dignified as she could, in her outsized, old faded shirt and baggy trousers and glared. "If you'd ever cleaned up this pigpen I wouldn't have had to throw all those old oily rags and papers in the stove!" She made an angry gesture. "It doesn't even look like the same kitchen. When was the last time you washed those walls or chipped the oily charcoal from your stove?" She ran out of breath. They glared at each other until Whit went to the table and sat down.

In a calmer voice he said, "Lizzie, I was up at the leather shop when the blacksmith came in an' said there was black smoke risin' from the stovepipe." He turned to look at her. "Suppose someone had thought it was a flue fire and come bustin' in here?"

She was perspiring, her cheek was smudged, and her hands were oily black. She breathed deeply several times, then matched his calmer tone of voice. "I had no idea that would happen. I was just trying to clean your house. If I have to stay cooped up in here until nightfall, I might as well be doing something."

He gestured toward a chair across from him. She went to it and leaned on the table. They looked at each other for a moment, then she arose, disappeared in the bedroom, and returned with his holstered Colt and shellbelt. As she dropped them atop the table she said, "Put it on. You looked conspicious when you left this morning. Everyone else in Beaverton is wearing a gun." She sat down as he ignored the gun and belt to gaze across at her. "Lizzie, you like to gave me heart failure."

She went to the drainboard for a towel and returned as she wiped her hands until most of the dirt and grease were gone. "I'm sorry, Whit. I suppose I should have realized oily rags and papers would make black smoke."

He held out a hand for the towel, then arose to lean across and rub off the smudge on her cheek. As he sat back down he smiled. "It sure makes a difference, don't it?"

"Yes. Have you ever washed these walls?"

He hadn't. "Now and then the stove. The walls—by golly, it looks lighter in here."

"Get married," she told him. "Get someone to look after you."

He felt around for his cut plug and under her impassive gaze skived off a cud and tucked into his cheek. As he was putting the plug and knife away she said, "On second thought, maybe you'd better not get married. I've never known a woman who could put up with *that*."

He stopped masticating and gazed stonily at her for a long time before replying. "Me gettin' married was your idea, Lizzie, not mine. I don't figure to get married. I've known a lot of men who did it. No thanks."

She arose without another word, returned from the stove with two sparkling clean cups with aromatic coffee in them, and as she pushed a cup in his direction she said, "Can I get away tonight?"

He closed both hands around the cup for its warmth and inhaled the aroma while nodding his head. "You better make it tonight. Another day like this one an' another night like last night an' I'll start havin' fits." He tasted the coffee, drank the cup half-empty, and leaned back. "You give me gray hairs, but I'm goin' to miss you. Tell you what, Lizzie, maybe you could lie over for another day or two and go over the rest of the house."

She knew exactly how to change the subject. "I took the money out of the commode pot."

His eyes widened. "What did you do with it?"

"You are sitting on it. It's stuck to the underside of your chair. You said no one would look under the bed. If I was looking for something that's the first place I'd look. The last place would be the underside of a kitchen chair."

He arose, lifted the chair, looked beneath it, put it back down, and sat on it. She said nothing throughout all this, but the moment he was sitting opposite her again she said, "How are you going to give it back?"

He had not thought about that. "Well, maybe just walk past the bank and fling it through the door."

Her brows ran together. "In broad daylight?"

"All right. How do I get it back?"

"Where does the bank gets its mail?"

"In Coggins's store. They got a little cubbyhole with a

bunch of boxlike pigeon nests against the wall. Everyone gets their mail . . ."

She smiled as his eyes widened. "You *mail* it to the bank."

He wagged his head. "Lizzie, you can't mail a letter in there that Walt and his clerk don't see every envelope an' remember 'em. There aren' no more'n fifteen, twenty letters sent out of here a week."

"All right. You go in, buy something—a plug of tobacco—and walk out leaving the envelope on the counter."

He pondered a moment, then shrugged heavy shoulders. "Maybe. I got plenty of time to figure that out. First off, I got to get rid of you."

She said, "Yes," in a very small voice and faced away from him.

He watched her profile and felt like kicking himself. "I didn't mean it like it sounded."

"Yes, you did. I don't blame you. They'd run you out of town on a greased pole if they knew you were helping me. I'm sorry I stayed and involved you. I should have just started walking after nightfall."

He snorted. "Walking? You wouldn't have got five miles."

"I could've stolen a horse."

"Yeah. And you'd have got shot. Care for another cup of coffee?" He was arising as he spoke.

She finally looked him in the face again. "Thank you, yes. Whit?"

"What?"

". . . Nothing. Be careful, the handle is hot."

21

Dusk and Beyond

SHE fed him supper, and when he wanted to help clean up afterward she snapped at him, "Just go see if it's dark enough yet. I want to get away from here early enough to have all night to travel."

As he left the house he wondered at her sudden changes of mood and decided that after all she had been through lately, she was probably entitled to seem a little wistful one moment and ready to claw like a cat the next.

It was a balmy evening and would be a warm night. At least until shortly before dawn. Beaverton was beginning to do as it usually did, taper off its commercial affairs and get ready for supper, and after that maybe, for married folks, a little pinochle or maybe reading; for the unattached men, a few games of pool, a drink or two, some visiting at Doughbelly's bar.

The blacksmith had closed up shop after banking the forge fire. Across the road one of Spooner's men was leading a tired big-necked buggy mare inside after freeing her from the shafts, and dumping the light harness in the back of the buggy.

Whit knew the rig and looked northward across Main Street to locate Carl Muller, who owned the big Oregon mare and the top-buggy. He was not in sight, but there was a light over at Given's jailhouse office. Whit studied that with increasing curiosity. It certainly was not Jack over there, and as far as Whit knew there had been no trouble in town today.

He had time to kill, so he crossed over, heard a gruff voice before reaching the door, and walked into brilliant light from a hanging lamp whose glass mantle was so clean it glistened.

There were two men in the office. One was slovenly, unshorn, with cracked old run-over boots, a gunless hip holster, and a bleary-eyed look. He was seated on a bench against the north wall.

Behind the desk a large, darkly bearded individual wearing Given's badge was examining a scarred old worn-out Colt six-gun that hadn't had even a hint of bluing on it for many years. The bearded man looked up as Whit entered, put down the old weapon, and said, "Good evening. Town council appointed me to fill in until Mister Given is back on his feet." As he finished saying this, Buffler Stoneman jutted his jaw. "That's my first prisoner."

Whit looked at the rangeman. He did not look like much of a prisoner. "What'd he do?"

"Earlier, he tried to pass some counterfeit coins over at Coggins's store an' later he tried the same thing at the saloon an' got run out of town. Later, he come back and tried the same thing over at the café."

Whit finished studying the disreputable-looking cowboy as Stoneman took down a copper circlet with keys attached and herded his prisoner down into the cell room to one of the strap-steel cages down there. When he returned, Whit was standing thoughtfully in front of the stove. He had taken this position unconsciously out of habit, because the evening was not cool and the stove was not burning.

As Stoneman went behind the table that served as a desk and tossed aside the key-ring, he picked up the old gun. "It's a good thing they made 'em with plenty of steel. Look at this. It's been used to drive nails, crack rocks, twist wire tight . . ." Stoneman put the gun down. "Mister Holt is goin' to start the southbound coaches moving again." Stoneman, who was a large, big-boned, rather massive individual, sat down and groaned. "I guess the lady outlaw got away. Posse-men went through town like coon dogs, lookin' for sign of her. Doughbelly said there was some woman tracks in the alley behind his place, but they're gone now. Too many wagons been up and down over there."

Stoneman eased back a little tentatively. This was not his first encounter with a chair he did not trust. But the chair held. He had one thing to add. "I was a deputy over in Idaho, and once I was a town marshal up north. Other times I been roped into ridin' with posses, but Mister Pierson, I got to tell you, in my experience this is the first time a robber didn't run, but turned right back into a town and somehow slid through the cracks an' didn't get caught."

Whit had a question. "Has everyone given up?"

Stoneman became defensive. "Well, it's been a while, you know. Shucks, by now she could be thirty miles away in the westerly mountains, even if she just walked away from here. Or—and Mister Bonner scoffed at me for saying this over at the bank—maybe she's got one hell of a friend here in town who is goin' to keep her hid out for as long as it takes."

Whit also scoffed, probably with less conviction than Charley Bonner had done, but Stoneman did not notice. "Three days, Buffler. If no one tracked her out of town, why then she must have left on horseback. There was too much excitement in town for someone to hide her this long." Whit pondered that statement, then added a little to it. "At least that's the way it seems to me."

The newly appointed temporary town marshal, like just about everyone else in Beaverton, tired of this subject easily and quickly. He mentioned something that had nothing to do with the lady outlaw. "Mister Holt is short a driver and a gun-guard. He didn't like the notion of me fillin' in for Mister Given."

Whit looked a little sour. "Hell, he never paid for a gun-guard if he could figure a way to weasel out of it. As for a driver, let him run crippled for a while. There are drivers around."

Stoneman regarded Whit from very dark eyes, then shot up to his feet. "It's suppertime. I'd be glad to have you come over to the café with me."

Whit declined, but walked out with Stoneman. He waited until the large man was across the road, then went up to the leather works. The door was locked, there was no light, and the town blacksmith called over from in front of the saloon to say that Hart had gone up to look in on Jack Given.

Whit threw a wave and started northward, but slowly. His purpose since leaving his house was to kill time, to wait for full darkness, and to take the pulse of the town as he waited.

One obvious thing was that life and routines were just about back to normal. Undoubtedly the depositors who had lost money as a result of the bank robbery were just as bitter as ever, but even they had businesses to operate or chores to do.

Whit did not go all the way up to the Muller place. He crossed to the east side of Main Street as he neared there and started southward. By the time he got as far down as the general store, it was softly dark and becoming increasingly so each passing moment.

He paused to watch a yardman appear at the corralyard gates and light the lanterns. Farther southward, near the lower extremity of town, the livery-barn lanterns were already glowing. Jake Spooner was wavily visible through the unclean café window, gorging at the counter among a herd of other diners.

Whit continued his stroll as far as the smithy and stepped down the darkest side of the sooty little building to watch Spooner's nightman dragging the chair with him as he lighted runway lamps.

That was where he had to get the horse for her.

He carved a chew off his plug, cheeked it, put up the plug,

and waited until the nighthawk took his old chair and went into the combination office and harness room.

The idea of stealing a horse was only mildly troublesome. He justified it by imagining how happy Spooner would be when he heard the money, part of which was his, had been returned to the bank.

The real danger was not particularly in stealing a horse, it was in getting caught for being involved with her at all. He put that out of his mind, too, looked northward up the empty roadway, and crossed to the area of old pole corrals north of the livery barn. As yet, he had done nothing that could not be easily explained, but nevertheless his heart was pounding as he kept most of the corral network between himself and the livery barn, although he did not expect the nightman to leave the comfort of the harness room. He studied horses as he moved along. It had to be an animal that would not buck her off half a mile from town, and it could not be a horse that would run away with her or do some other irritating thing. Horse traders were traditionally sly, devious, untrustworthy individuals, so there was no telling what kind of stock Spooner had.

He heard someone clumping down the plankwalk and crouched until the person had passed. The pear-shaped physique identified the walker as Jake Spooner. Whit was beginning to warily straighten up when the nightman walked back the way Jake had come, cut across the road, and entered the café.

Jake emerged from the rear of his barn, smoking a cigar. He strolled toward the nearest corral to look in on the horses, perhaps to make certain his nighthawk had fed them.

Whit sank to the ground in a crouch. He could infrequently see the liveryman as the horses between them moved. Spooner paused across the way, hooked a boot over the lowest stringer, removed his cigar, and said, "Red, you're goin' to be my personal horse. Someday someone'll come along and

I'll get a hunnert dollars for you. Until then, I'm the only one that'll ride you."

Whit singled out the horse Spooner had spoken to. He looked to be seal-brown in the darkness, not a particularly tall horse, maybe a hair under fifteen hands, but he was built from the ground up, with muscles where other horses didn't even have creases. He also had a good head, and while Jake had been speaking to him, he eyed the man with a calm expression while chewing bits of timothy he'd lipped up.

Whit made a guess about his age. Maybe six or seven. Maybe eight or nine. All good ages. He spat out his cud, and when Spooner went strolling back to the barn, cigar letting off little gray puffs of smoke, thick thumbs hooked nonchalantly in his suspenders, Whit stood up very slowly to begin working his way soundlessly around where he could make a judgment of the horse he thought was a seal-bay. He found that he was in fact a blood-bay, his color clearly defined, not rusty like some blood-bays.

Again, the red horse raised his head without a trace of uneasiness and eyed the man looking in at him. Whit smiled, held out his palm, and when the red horse stretched its neck to sniff, Whit winked at him.

He could have bad habits. Lots of imperturbable, reliable-seeming horses had bad habits, but Whit would have bet his best hat this horse had none.

Whit lingered over there until the nightman returned from supper and the roadway was empty again, then crossed the road, went back to his house, and walked in to find one lamp lighted, turned down as low as the wick would go, and the curly-headed, dark-eyed woman sitting at the kitchen table.

She offered no greeting; she simply said, "Well?"

He shook the coffeepot, filled a cup, and took it to the table with him as he told her about the blood-bay gelding. When he had finished and was drinking lukewarm coffee, she had another question for him. "How do you get it over here, and do I ride bareback or on a saddle?"

He finished the coffee, put the cup aside, leaned on the table, and looked at her and said, "I don't get it over here. We go over there. I've got some bridles in a closet, but I don't have a saddle. It's up at the corralyard. If I go up there tonight and—"

"I understand."

"Can you ride bareback?"

"I grew up riding bareback."

"Yes. Well, this time you might have to do it for a hell of lot of miles."

She brought something up from her lap. He watched her put it atop the table. It looked like a brown-paper parcel that contained something more or less round. There was writing on it, but he had to turn up the lamp to read it. Afterward, he raised his face to her. She said, "It's all rolled up in there. Eight thousand dollars. I thought about it while you were gone. It would look better if my handwriting was on it. It might not make any difference, but my handwriting is bound to be different from yours. Anyone who sees lots of writing, like a banker for instance, will know a woman addressed it."

She stood up. He noticed the bulge inside his old work shirt as she was speaking. "I'm ready any time you are."

"You'll need grub," he told her, rising from the table, but she was ahead of him here too. "I have enough in my—your—trouser pockets . . . Whit? Once we walk out of here I might not have a chance to say this: I'll owe you as long as I live. . . . I wish I hadn't robbed the bank, then I could stay in Beaverton . . . clean your coffeepot now and then, and make biscuits for you that don't set like lead."

He stood, gazing at her in the unstable light, unable to think of a single nice thing to say back to her.

She walked around, grabbed his shoulders, stood on tiptoes, yanked him lower, and kissed him squarely on the mouth, very hard, then she moved swiftly to the door and, with a hand on the latch, gave him an order.

"Get a bridle."

He got it from the closet in the bedroom. When he returned to the kitchen the door was ajar and she was waiting outside. He scooped up the brown-paper parcel and forced it into a pocket as he hastened to join her.

Beaverton was quiet; it was past bedtime for most of its inhabitants. When she started briskly forward, he grabbed her arm and growled at her.

Horsemen were coming into town from the south. He waited until they passed. When she raised her eyebrows questioningly he said, "Three hostlers from the stage-company yard. The feller who owns the company's got six or seven hundred acres southeast of town where he keeps spare horses and ones that need rest. He usually sends yardmen down there about every couple of weeks to look things over." As he finished speaking, he led her to the corner of the smithy and pointed up where three riders were entering the corralyard past the flickering carriage lamps.

The road was empty, a few lights still glowed, but most of Beaverton was dark. He stood motionless for so long she dug him with her elbow. He pointed beyond the corrals to a pair of moving shadows in the alley.

They watched those two silhouettes enter the barn from out back. Whit cursed to himself, but when the nighthawk appeared in the runway to greet the newcomers, his anxiety was put to rest.

"About time you got down here. Did you remember the bottle? Come on, I got the table cleared off an' the cards ready."

All three men disappeared inside the combination office and harness room.

22

By Starshine

CROSSING the road caused Whit and Lizzie a moment of anxiety, but darkness helped, as did the distance from the upper section of town to the lower end.

He led her eastward to a trash-littered area of weeds, beyond that to the alley, stopped briefly, then took her alongside the corrals. The only time they froze was when a dog barked behind them westerly, but no one seemed to heed the noise, so after a while they moved carefully among the corrals until they were over where the blood-bay was. The horse was on the far side, dozing. Whit pointed him out to the woman, then retraced his steps until he got around there. The horse knew they were approaching. When they reached him he was placidly watching them.

Whit had the bridle draped from a shoulder. Not every loose horse could be bridled without first being tied.

Lizzie looked the animal over as Whit jackknifed between pole stringers and straightened up very slowly inside the corral.

Several horses sidled warily away but the blood-bay did not move. Whit raised a hand very slowly and spoke. The horse stretched his neck to smell the hand, which he had smelled recently enough for Whit to seem familiar.

The horse looked past where Lizzie was watching, and turned back only when Whit took several slow steps ahead, hand a little higher to stroke the horse's neck. The blood-bay sucked back a little but still did not give ground.

Whit stood like a stone for a long time, listening, looking around, waiting to ease up again. The other animals in the corral were watching on the far side.

Lizzie whispered. Whit refused to be distracted, so she came through the stringers and pressed something into his hand. He did not have to look, he could smell it—it was an apple.

This time the bay horse nuzzled Whit's arm, tracing out the aroma. When he found the apple Whit held it so that he could take a bite but not get the whole apple. The horse came forward while still chewing. Whit slowly unwound the bridle reins, and as the horse reached for the remains of the apple, he very gently draped the reins over the horse's neck and held them loosely.

The horse chewed apple, and while of course he knew he had been caught, he did nothing to indicate protest. He was still chewing when Whit told Lizzie to go back to the alley gate and keep the other animals from coming out when he led the blood-bay into the alley.

A sudden burst of loud profanity erupted from inside the livery barn, followed by loud laughter. Lizzie did not open the gate until the noise subsided. As she did so, flagging at the horses that were following the bay to keep them from also coming out, she hissed at Whit. "Did you hear a door slam?"

He hadn't heard anything. He was shaking his head as he led the blood-bay out and waited until Lizzie was closing the gate before he bridled the horse; he had to take up slack in both cheek pieces before the bit hung properly. He also had to snug up the curb strap.

A man hacked violently and expectorated. The noise was loud enough to have been heard across Main Street. Whit twisted to seek the origin of the racket. Lizzie pointed toward the rear doorless opening of the barn, where someone was silhouetted by runway light as he pulled out a big old red bandanna and lustily blew his nose.

Whit shoved the reins into Lizzie's hand, said, "Wait," and reached the corral network with four big strides. He went southward, pressing close to the corrals. On his left, curious animals crowded up. Their movement masked Whit's movement.

The noisy individual in the barn doorway roughly shoved his handkerchief away, looked at the sky, then shuffled northward as far as the side of the barn and turned his back. He should have seen Lizzie up there in the middle of the alley holding a bridled horse, but evidently he did not see her because he neither faltered in his stride nor stopped to stare.

He also did not hear Whit sneak up behind him and strike him on the head. He went down like a poleaxed bull.

When Whit got back to Lizzie he leaned on the horse's left side, cupped his hands, and she raised a foot. Lizzie came down astraddle the horse gently and at once evened up the reins. Whit said, "Go! An' don't stop except to blow the horse until you are ten miles along. Then you can slack off because you got to favor that horse, but don't stop until you're in those westerly mountains."

She turned her head instinctively. "What's over there?"

"Mountains! Go, Lizzie, that man's not goin' to sleep forever. If he hadn't come out no one would have missed the horse until morning. Ride steady, Lizzie, not fast. Now go!"

She was holding her rein hand inches above the bloodbay's withers as she looked down at him, no longer making any attempt to hide the wistfulness. "Whit?"

He stepped back and slapped the blood-bay smartly on the rump. She had to grab the mane hair. The horse passed the lighted runway in two bounds. He was down among the tarpaper shacks at the lowest extremity of Beaverton and still moving right along when Whit heard the man he'd hit on the head make a groan.

Lizzie needed all the time she could get. Whit walked quickly down to where the man was unsteadily trying to push up onto all fours, hit him again, stepped over him, and hurried to Main Street.

He could no longer hear a loping horse. In the runway someone yelled a name. Whoever was looking for the missing cardplayer was irritated. He called several times, then swore.

Whit also wanted to swear. His idea had been for Lizzie to have at least a five-hour headstart. She still might get it, but it began to appear less of a certainty when another voice echoed over in the runway.

Someone was walking toward the alley carrying a lantern. Whit moved over as far as the smithy and stood in darkness to watch.

He began to seriously worry when the lantern was placed on the ground alongside the barn and men's astonished voices reached him.

He recognized one voice when Jake Spooner's nighthawk said, "Go get that big feller with the black beard who is acting marshal." In response to a murmur, the nightman spoke even louder. "How the hell do I know where he is? Try the roomin' house, the jailhouse. Raise a howl until you locate him."

There was another murmur, and this time the nightman was slower replying. "We was just havin' a friendly little poker session to pass the time. Jake won't care. Now for crissake, go find the marshal . . . I got no idea, Hiram. Until he comes around an' tells us, there's no way for us to know. Go, damn it, *go get the marshal!*"

Evidently the man called Hiram departed, because there was no further conversation. Whit looked at the moon, looked southward out of town, then westward. She needed more time. Maybe it would take that unconscious man half an hour or so to be roused. One thing was sure: that poker player was going to have the granddaddy of all headaches.

Whit tucked a cud into his cheek, heard Spooner's nighthawk complaining loudly as he struggled to get the injured man up the runway to the harness room, and had an abrupt, desperate idea.

He forgot to squeeze his cud as he intently watched the struggling nightman. Obviously the injured man was unable to help much as the nightman tried to support him and lead him at the same time. It further hindered the nightman's panting effort that the injured man was easily sixty pounds heavier than the nighthawk.

Whit looked northward up the dark, empty road, saw no one, and sprinted back over among the corrals, startling dozing horses who milled in fright, raising dust and making noise. He had to ignore the ruckus as he went swiftly to the burning lantern that had been left out back, scooped it up by the bale as he continued to move, spilled coal oil clear of the runway in the dusty alleyway, then dropped the lantern. The mantle shattered, flames caught, feebly at first, then began rising higher as they sent up pungent black smoke.

He looked up the runway, saw the struggling nighthawk try to turn while supporting his companion, so Whit sprang southward out of sight.

The nighthawk squawked, dropped his friend, and ran to a wall to snatch a broad-nosed manure shovel. While his back was to the flames Whit jumped inside, vaulted a stall door, and crouched. He peered around apprehensively, but there was no animal in there with him, which was very good fortune.

He heard the nightman running toward the alley, raised up when he ran past, jumped back over the door, and as the nightman frantically tried to shovel enough dust from the alleyway to smother the fire, Whit hurried to the inert injured man, flopped him over, plundered his pockets, held everything he got in both hands, and raced for the front barn entrance. He did not look back until he could do so from beside the front doorway. The nighthawk was still frantically shoveling, with his back to the barn's interior, scuffling up clouds of light-limned dirt and dust.

Whit heard hurrying footfalls northward, guessed who might be making them, and ducked around the lower side of the barn to wait. When the footfalls turned down the runway, he looked northward, saw no one, and sprinted back to the concealment of the smithy.

He was breathless, his heart was pounding, and there was sweat running under his shirt. Across the road loud voices held his attention as he pulled down big sweeps of air. The fire was out, three men moved back up into the lighted runway, and Whit recognized the largest of the three as Buffler Stoneman.

There was nothing more he could do. His idea had been spur-of-the-moment, probably flawed, but if it accomplished nothing more than confusion in town, he would be satisfied. Confusion would provide Lizzie with a little more time. Along with darkness, it just might provide her with all the time she needed to reach the mountains.

He went around back to his house, dumped the items from the injured man's plundered pockets atop the kitchen table, and without lighting a lamp, leaned down to sort through the usual articles such as a clasp knife, an old dented watch, a lint-encrusted plug of tobacco, some silver coins, and a small wad of crumpled greenbacks. He pushed it all into a sack, hid it at the bottom of the kindling box, and washed his face and hands in cold water before groping in a dark cupboard for his bottle of whiskey. He sat at the table and sipped liquor until his heart was back to normal and his nerves had stopped crawling.

He did not even think of bedding down. He could not have slept if he had, so he took a final rinse of popskull, stowed the bottle, and went outside to stand in darkness, listening.

If there was activity over at Spooner's livery, he could not hear it. He watched a ghostly, ragged cloud pass across the face of the moon and continue on its way.

He sat on a weathered bench against the house and thought about the handsome woman with black curly hair and eyes like obsidian. Would she make it? How far would she go before she stopped fleeing? Hopefully, damned far. Only when he had to shift weight did he feel the thick wad in his pocket. Until this moment he had completely forgotten it.

In the morning, or maybe about noon when most folks would be having dinner, he'd go up to the store and leave the little bundle for Walt Coggins to find and give to Charley Bonner.

Of one thing he was certain, no horsemen left town riding southward or he would have heard. He had not thought they would; so far as he knew people believed Lizzie had escaped days earlier. But even if possemen had ridden out of town on a manhunt, they could not make haste while walking along leading horses, trying to track someone by starshine. As time passed he began to feel more reassured and relaxed.

There was a bite to the air. Whit went back inside, and by now the whiskey's cumulative effect was beginning to combine with his exhaustion to make him feel very tired. Finally he went to bed.

But it was a very short night. In what seemed only moments after closing his eyes, someone shaping steel over an anvil at the smithy out front wakened him. It was morning, but he did not feel rested as he swung to his feet. He did not feel pleased with much of anything he had done over the past few days until a hand brushed against that hard packet in his pocket. Then he smiled. If they never found their bank robber it would matter a hell of a lot less after they got their money back.

He went to wash, shave, and head for the café. He was not hungry, but the caféman's little cubbyhole surpassed even Doughbelly's saloon as a fount of the latest news and gossip.

23

Excitement in Town

TOM Hart was up at the café, as was the blacksmith and his muscular helper. So was Walt Coggins, seated at the counter beside Charley Bonner, who still did not have good color. Charley only ate at the café when his wife was out of town.

Sam Holt looked up when his former whip walked in, peered to make a positive indentification, then bobbed his head and went back to his meal.

Carl Muller had left a few minutes earlier, but that did not matter, because as soon as Whit found a seat the man beside him said, "Jack's on the mend. Carl says he'll be up an' down for a while but he ain't going to die."

On Whit's other side someone nudged him and said, "You slept through the excitement last night. Jake's nightman an' three of his drinkin' friends was havin' a poker game in the harness room. One of 'em went out back to pee and someone knocked him over the head and robbed him."

Sam Holt finished breakfast, put down some silver, and on his way out paused behind Whit to say, "Ten dollars more'n I paid you, Whit. I need a driver real bad."

The answer Holt got was not as curt as the other ones he'd gotten earlier for speaking along these lines. "I'll be up directly an' we'll talk."

Holt left the café, pausing in the morning sunlight to polish his glasses before walking briskly in the direction of his corralyard.

When Whit had finished and went out front, Tom Hart

was waiting for him. Neither of them said anything until Whit had his morning chew in place, a ritual Hart watched with a pinched-down expression of disapproval, but when he spoke it was not about Whit's habit.

"Jake is runnin' around down yonder like a man with his britches full of ants. Someone stole a horse off him. Most likely it was last night. The way Buffler Stoneman's got it figured, they started a little fire in the back alley to keep Jake's nightman busy shoveling dirt, and made off with the horse durin' the excitement."

Whit arched an amber spray into the roadway, then said, "The hell. Well, if he got their attention by lighin' a fire out in the alley, then sure as hell that's one direction he didn't escape in."

The harness maker mused about that and cleared his throat. Whit knew a disagreement was coming, so he spoke first. "Tom, could it have been the lady outlaw?" he asked, and waved an arm northward. "There's a lot of open country up there before she can reach any kind of cover. But if she had all night to do it in . . ."

Hart squinted up the roadway. "Yeah. But if you're thinkin' of makin' up a band to go after her, leave me out."

Whit gazed at the taller, rawboned man. "Why?"

Hart brought his gaze back to the storefronts across from the café. "I already told you, partner. I just don't have the time to go traipsin' all over the country like we done last week. I got a business to run." Hart put a direct gaze upon Whit "Let Buffler do it. He wants to be the town marshal. Let him cut his teeth on this one. He'll never find her if she can get into them mountains. Jake said whoever robbed his corral stole the best horse he owned." Hart reached inside his shirt to scratch. "See you later," he said, and walked away.

Whit went up to visit with Doughbelly. When he walked into the almost empty saloon, Buffler Stoneman turned from the counter where he and Doughbelly had been talking. When Whit crossed over, Doughbelly said, "Beer? Me'n

Mister Stoneman been talkin' about that mystery down at your end of town."

Whit nodded about the beer, and as Doughbelly departed to draw it off Whit turned toward Stoneman. "Mystery?"

Stoneman shifted against the counter. "That's what Doughbelly calls it. Someone knocked a feller over the head at the livery barn last night, robbed him, then started a little fire in the alley."

Whit considered his face in the wavery backbar mirror. "Don't sound like a mystery to me."

Stoneman's reply was pensive. "Well, last night someone stole Spooner's best horse too. Them things happened about the same time. Now then, it comes out about like this— someone on foot waylaid that man beside the barn an' robbed him, an' most likely they stole the horse to get away on." Stoneman waited until Doughbelly set the glass in front of Whit before continuing. "What sticks in my craw, Mister Pierson, is why in hell did he light that little fire? A robber an' horsethief don't want to attract attention to himself. I can't figure out why the damned fool lit the fire."

Whit considered his beer. "One thing, Marshal. He couldn't have gone south. Not one horse out of a thousand could be made to ride through a fire. One horse in a million, maybe."

Doughbelly gazed admiringly at Whit. "That's right. Sure as hell, he went north."

Stoneman smiled a little flintily. "Yeah," he said. "I know that. I had a little trouble talkin' 'em into it, but I got four town possemen scouring the country northward." Stoneman shook his head. "Still don't make much sense the thief just happened to see that feller up against the side of the barn, maybe while he was sneakin' the horse out of Spooner's corral, an' decided to rob him on the spot. The feller he hit over the head told me he'd lost nine dollars in the poker game before he went out back and didn't have more'n about another two dollars in his pockets."

Whit smiled. "The robber wouldn't know that, would he? He just saw a chance, took it, and didn't get very much." It was close to noon according to the back bar clock. Whit left the saloon, watched Sam Holt's yardmen backing a hitch onto the pole of a coach, and turned southward toward the general store. As he passed the bank Charley Bonner intercepted him. Charley's smile of greeting was grim. "There was trouble in town again last night. I don't know what's getting into folks. It's getting so's a person'll have to start locking his doors and packing a gun all the time."

Whit nodded without commenting.

Bonner's eyes settled steadily on Whit. "Sam's in a bad way, Whit."

He got another nod and no comment.

"Didn't neither one of us deliberately set out to get you into trouble by sneaking that money down here. In fact, Sam wanted me to pay for a guard to ride with you. I didn't figure it was necessary, an' I also figured that if anyone saw you driving along with a guard on the seat with you, they'd know there was something valuable on your coach."

Whit did not nod again, he smiled. "Cost both of you, didn't it? I'm goin' over to talk to Sam directly." He stared at the banker. "You were down at the café this morning."

Bonner sighed. "Yes. My wife's cousin down in Center City got sick last week. She went down to look after her."

"Sure hope the lady gets well soon," Whit said, and would have walked on but the banker stopped him. "Sam's eyesight is getting pretty bad. He's got to get someone over there with him who can help run things."

"He hasn't been able to see worth a damn since I've known him."

"But he's worse lately. Carl says there isn't a blessed thing that can be done. Sam always put great store by you, Whit."

Whit left. A few yards farther along he paused to look back. The bank doorway was empty. He reset his hat and continued strolling as far as the dog-trot between the general store and the empty structure south of it.

He walked slower, looked, saw no one close except two old men arguing across the road with their backs to him, so he stepped into the dog-trot, followed it to the alley, and before moving out, made certain no one was in sight. His heart was pounding again. If helping an outlaw was the same as *being* one, a man, and maybe a woman as well, had to be crazy to get into that line of work. It was too hard on the constitution.

He did not like doing this in broad daylight, but neither did he like carrying that bundle in his pocket; right now, because he was satisfied Lizzie had gotten far enough away to be safe, there only remained getting shed of the damned stolen money. Then he'd go over and talk to Sam. He sidled up in the direction of the Bonner house, watching over his shoulder and in all other directions as he went along.

If he was seen leaving that package at Bonner's house, he might just as well steal another horse and hightail it exactly as Lizzie had done.

The Bonner residence was one of a handful of pretentious homes in the Beaverton countryside. It was two stories high with elegant curlicues for door, window, and porch trim. And it was painted; most other houses around town were either not painted at all or had been whitewashed, which was a lot cheaper. The Bonner place had a handsome, wide covered porch that ran completely around the place, and there was tall shrubbery mixed with flowers and young trees, some of the trees flowering varieties. Charley's wife had spent money over the years, making her home one of the most elegant around.

On the alley side the yard had a seven-feet-tall solid wooden fence to insure privacy; elsewhere shrubbery accomplished somewhat the same purpose but in a manner that would not antagonize the neighbors.

Whit passed from the alley to the area of thickest shrubbery directly south of the back door, which was shaded by the porch overhang. He crouched there for a long time, listening to sounds behind him, studying the residences to the east beyond the hedges, and telling himself that with his luck, the moment he stepped clear and raced for the back porch, a neighbor would emerge from one of the nearby houses. But he sprinted anyway, and except for a barking dog that turned up about the time Whit reached the porch, it seemed that he had made a successful crossing.

The back door was bolted but a kitchen window south of it was not. Whit raised it, shook off sweat, stepped inside, and had to wait a moment for his erratic heartbeat to become less wild, then passed from the kitchen to the dining room, placed the bundle on the round oak table, blew out a ragged breath, and retreated back to the window. As he climbed out and lowered the sash, that dog started up again.

Whit stepped off the edge of the porch, ducked into some flowering lilac bushes whose perfume was almost overpowering, and did not move until someone beyond the Bonner yard called angrily at the dog.

When it seemed safe to leave the lilac bushes Whit used both arms to push through. The alley gate was about a hundred feet dead ahead. He stood a long time, listening, looking, and fervently hoping, then made the dash.

The dog did not bark again as he got through the gate into the alley. He was very careful to use concealment until he was as far southward as Coggins's store, then he walked in plain sight, moving casually until he came to another dog-trot that took him back to Main Street.

Here, finally, with Beaverton's normal midday activities proceeding in their normal way, he leaned on wood siding near the dog-trot and breathed deeply, his nerves still quivering, but with an almost euphoric sensation of final accomplishment calming his heart and providing him with a great sense of relief.

It was done. It was finished. It was all over, finally.

Doctor Muller emerged from Coggins's store with a small

package, saw Whit standing there, and nodded to him. "I expect you know about what happened last night," he said, halting to gaze thoughtfully at his friend. "It don't make much sense. Horsethieves don't build fires while they're robbing people and stealing animals."

Whit agreed. "No they don't. I couldn't figure that either."

Muller's shrewd gray eyes narrowed slightly as he studied Whit. "You been running?"

"No. Why?"

"Because you're sweating and it's not that hot out, and the pulse in that big vein in the side of your neck is pumping pretty fast."

Whit made a little smile. "Got a little upset stomach is all."

Muller did not appear to have heard that. He was studying Whit with a little more interest. "You didn't get a haircut, did you?"

"No."

"Odd. You smell of that French lilac water the barber uses. Well, I've got to get back up yonder."

"How is he doing, Carl?"

"Jack? He sure confounded me. For the amount of blood around him up there in the road where he got shot, and on his clothing, I wouldn't have bet a plugged penny he'd make it. But, by golly, this morning he was hungry. Ravenous in fact. That's the best of all symptoms of recovery. But it'll be a while, Whit. Maybe a month or more."

Whit watched Muller cross through roadway dust, walking with his head down like a man in thought. He decided he needed something stronger than coffee and reversed himself, went up to the Waterhole Saloon, and when Doughbelly brought a glass of beer Whit drank the glass empty. As Doughbelly went to refill it, Whit felt sweat breaking out all over and mopped his face before Doughbelly returned.

Evidently Doughbelly did not think the perspiration was unusual, because he said, "Gettin' to be that time of year again. Spring's past an' summer is nigh."

Whit told him what Doctor Muller had said about the marshal and Doughbelly beamed. He went to draw off two glasses this time, and when he returned he raised his glass. "That's the best news I've heard in a long time."

They drank and Whit departed, heading for home. He was opposite the abstract office near the lower end of town when a commotion broke out back up north of the general store. Like everyone else who heard it, he turned.

Charley Bonner and his bank clerk were in the doorway, gesturing and shouting like crazy men. Whit was too distant to make out what they were yelling about, but passersby who were closer seemed galvanized by whatever it was and also began crying out and acting excited.

Wes came out of his shoeing shed with a pair of tongs in his fist, sweat-streaked dirty face contorted into an expression of angry apprehension as he moved clear of the plankwalk so he could see up in the direction of the bank. He could not make out what the noise was about either, but because Whit was a little closer he called to him.

"That damned bank been robbed again?"

Whit shrugged. "I don't know," he said, and watched the blacksmith start hurriedly up the road, shiny old muleskin apron flapping, still clutching the tongs.

Whit passed behind to his house, went inside, made a beeline for his kitchen cupboard, took the bottle to the table with him, and sat down, scowling at it. He had not expected that damned banker to find the bundle on his dining-room table so fast.

He took a rinse of whiskey. Charley must have been on his way home for some reason about the time Whit was entering that dog-trot where he emerged on Main Street and bumped into Carl Muller, and that, by gawd, had been too close. Suppose Whit had hesitated a little or Charley had come home sooner. Sure as hell he would have met Whit in his dining room with no believable excuse for being there.

He had another swallow of whiskey. The life of an outlaw,

even an unwilling, accidental one, would sooner or later sure as hell give a man a heart failure.

He took one more swallow, returned the bottle to its cupboard, and with a bucket in each hand went out to begin hauling bathwater. Maybe washing the nervous sweat off would help, along with the whiskey.

The racket up the road had subsided. As Whit hauled water he imagined townsfolk crowding inside the bank to gaze at the wad of returned greenbacks, eight thousand dollars' worth of them. Everybody would be laughing, relieved and thankful while Whit Pierson was hauling bathwater in a disgruntled mood with enough whiskey sloshing inside to appease his conscience, except that it did not do it. He still felt like a full-blown horse-thieving, conniving renegade.

24

Muller's Visit

WHEN Whit entered Sam Holt's office up at the corralyard, Sam had his desk lamp turned up, although it was well along toward high noon, and was holding a freight manifest close, squinting at it.

Sam lowered the paper, peered at his visitor, then put the paper aside and leaned forward with both elbows atop the littered desk as he said, "When I was over to Denver a couple years ago I saw a machine with metal arms stickin' up out of it, and when the lady hit a little button in front one of them arms reared up like a kicking grasshopper and hit a piece of paper an', by gawd, a letter appeared on the paper." Sam gestured toward the paper he'd put aside. "Someday, maybe, folks will use them machines to write with. Whoever filled out this manifest had real bad handwriting. One of them machines would have printed on that paper like a book. Easy to read."

Having said all this, Sam rose to his feet. "Care for a cup of coffee?"

Whit accepted the offer even though he did not want coffee. He sat down, and when Sam handed him the cup he said, "Thanks," and waited for Sam to go back behind his desk.

"Did you hear they got the money back over at the bank?" Sam asked.

Whit hadn't heard, but he nodded anyway. The coffee was hot and bitter.

"The lady outlaw left it up at Charley's house on a table."

"Was it all there?"

"Every blessed cent of it. Why do you expect she did that?"

Whit put the cup on a little table. "Maybe her conscience bothered her."

"Outlaws don't have consciences, Whit."

"Well then, you tell me why she did it."

Sam shrugged thin shoulders and changed the subject. "What with Buffler Stoneman acting as lawman until Jack can get back into harness, and one driver quit on me an' another drinkin' too much, I need another driver, Whit."

"Sounds like you need two more drivers, Sam."

"Yeah, but I'll hire 'em one at a time. What I said over at the café still goes—ten dollars more a month."

"And you tell me exactly what I'll be hauling every blessed time I take a coach out. And if it's money or the like, then you or somebody pays a gun-guard to go along."

Possibly Sam had anticipated something like this because he was nodding agreeably before Whit had finished speaking. "Agreed. Now then, will you roll out with the south-bound first thing in the morning?"

Whit nodded, left his coffee untouched, and went back out into the sunshine. Doughbelly was riding past with a bundle of shanks and halters lashed behind his cantle. When he saw Whit he said, "Goin' out to Flaherty's place and fetch back Spooner's horses. Want to ride along?"

Whit shook his head. "You're gettin' a late start."

Doughbelly smiled. "Yeah, I know. I figured it so's I'd reach the ranch about suppertime." He slapped a saddlebag, winked, and rode on past. That saddlebag bulged in the shape of a whiskey bottle.

Whit eyed the bank, where people were passing in and out. He looked in the opposite direction, where Coggins's store was also back to normal, and on the same side of the road, Tom Hart's harness and saddle works. He was considering going down to pass a little time with Tom when the acting town marshall came along. He asked if Whit had seen Doughbelly. When Whit told him where Doughbelly was headed, Buffler grinned. "Him and that old cowman got along real well, didn't they?"

Whit gazed at the big man. "Yeah. Why did she give the money back, Marshal?"

Stoneman became solemn and stroked his thick beard while responding. "Everybody's got some notion about that," he stated. "Me, it sticks in my craw that Mister Bonner's wife left town to go look after an ailin' cousin about the time that there lady outlaw was hiding out, and when her husband went home, there was the money wrapped in brown paper addressed to the bank."

Whit stared at the big man, uncertain whether he had picked up the correct implication from Stoneman's rambling statement. "You think Charley's wife was the outlaw?"

Stoneman stopped combing his beard. "Maybe. Mostly likely not. But my notion is that she hid the real outlaw. No one would think to search the banker's house, would they? Mister Pierson, there was the money, smack-dab in the center of Mister Bonner's dining-room table."

Whit did not blink in his regard of the town marshal. He said slowly, "Buffler, I don't think I'd spread that notion around town."

Stoneman nodded sagely. "Oh, I wouldn't do that. Mister Pierson, as far as I'm concerned the lady outlaw is gone, the money's back in Mister Bonner's vault, one of these days Missus Bonner will return, and that will be that. I was just headin' for the café—care to come along an' join me in a cup of coffee?"

"No, thanks. I'm about to float from coffee this morning."

Whit watched the large man angle over to the café and disappear inside. Evidently a beneficial offshoot of the money being returned was that the matter of someone stealing one of Jake Spooner's horses and robbing that harness-room poker player was almost forgotten.

Whit turned southward. As he passed the harness works and looked in, Tom did not raise his eyes from fitting a moist fork-leather over the naked horn of a saddle. Whit kept on walking, crossed over near the abstract office, and responded to a wave from the blacksmith on his way around back to his little house.

Carl Muller was dozing on the little bench near the door. He evidently heard someone coming, because he jerked awake and raised his head. Whit was too surprised to see him there to do more than stare until the doctor gathered himself to arise, then Whit said, "You hidin' out?"

Muller drew a voluminous white handkerchief from a coat pocket and mopped his eyes with it as he replied. "No. You got some coffee in the kitchen?"

Whit led the way inside, punched around to find coals in the stove, fed in some kindling, put the blueware pot atop a burner, and turned to find Muller studying him. "Nice day," Whit said, took down two tin cups, and carried them to the table with him.

The doctor agreed about the day, groped around until he found a cigar, and offered one to Whit, who declined. Muller bit off the end, struck a sulphur match that let go with a rank smelling cloud of smoke, and got his stogie fired up. He removed it, gazed steadily at Whit, and finally said, "Jack is doing fine."

Whit nodded about that. When he'd been at the stove he had begun feeling uncomfortable for some indefinable reason. They were friends, had been for a long time, but Muller hadn't ever waited out front of the house for him before. He said, "Somethin' I can help you with, Carl?"

Muller trickled bluish smoke without taking his eyes off Whit or replying for a long moment. "Well, maybe," he answered, shifting his gaze to the stove, the sink, to the drainboard, and the immaculate walls, before speaking again. "When we met yesterday out front of the general store . . ." Muller paused to consider cigar ash, then cleared his throat and started over. "In my business it's necessary to pay close attention to a man, otherwise I might diagnose croup when it's really lung fever."

Whit's discomfort increased as he watched the older man, who was very clearly being careful in his choice of words. But Whit was a direct individual, dissembling annoyed him. "Yeah, I expect you're right. Carl, spit it out."

Muller gestured around the room with his cigar hand. "You been doing spring cleaning, have you?"

Whit did not take his eyes off the older man. "A place needs goin' over now and then."

Muller smiled softly. "Yeah. Being a widower, I know. I been using the same cleaning lady for years." The cigar hand sank to the table. The shrewd gray eyes were fixed on Whit's face. "Something else," he said. "When we met yesterday you'd been running, or doing something that had you pretty well keyed up."

Whit was beginning to have a dawning suspicion, but he said nothing, simply sat there waiting for Muller to say more. It was not a very long wait.

"Whit, you ever seen that big stand of lilacs Charley's wife's got out back of their house? Damned things nearly take your breath away with their fragrance."

Whit's lips barely moved. "Like that toilet water the barber sprinkles on a man after a shave?"

Muller nodded. "The coffee's boiling."

Whit got the pot, filled both cups, returned the pot to the stove, and resumed his place at the table. "It'll be hot," he said.

The doctor ignored the coffee. His cigar had gone out, so he deftly trimmed off the ash with a finger and gently placed the cigar back into a coat pocket. When he caught Whit's look he said, "At two for a nickel a man can't just toss them away when they're only half smoked." He leaned on the table. "You got any idea how that money got on Charley's dining-room table?"

Whit pulled his cup in closer before answering. Without raising his head he knew Muller was staring at him. He continued to consider the tin cup as he replied, "Someone put it there." He looked up. "The main thing is, Carl, Charley got his money back."

"Yes. That's the main thing. Charley's pleased as punch. So is everyone else around town who had money in the bank. Including me. I suppose folks will let things slide now."

"But not you?"

"Well, sure, I'm willing too," Muller said, and tasted the coffee, tasted it again, and his eyes twinkled a little. "You even cleaned the coffee pot. Last time I had coffee here—"

"Carl, I said spit it out!"

"All right, but it's just a doctor's deduction. I'd like to know I'm not diagnosing lung fever for the croup . . . Did you hide her out down here?"

"Yes. Overnight."

"And she's gone now? Maybe on Jake's blood-bay horse?"

"Yes."

Muller eased back in his chair. "And you came out of the dog-trot smelling of lilacs because you put that money on Charley's table, then hightailed it through Charley's backyard by way of the lilac bushes?"

"Yes."

Muller gazed across the table for a moment before speaking again. "How did she come to give the money back?"

"We made a trade. When I walked in here and found her already in the house with a gun, she wanted to get away. I didn't stand a chance of getting the money without getting shot, so I made her an offer."

"You'd get a horse for her if she'd give back the money?"

"Exactly. I stole that horse from Jake's corral, knocked that man over the head for a diversion, set the fire in the alley to distract the nighthawk while I robbed the unconscious man so it would look like a robbery, and she left town riding southwesterly toward the mountains."

RIDERS OF THE TROJAN HORSE

Muller teetered his chair for a while, then brought it down so he could reach for the coffee cup. Whit watched everything he did, even when he raised the cup with twinkling eyes and made a mock salute with the cup before drinking from it. When he lowered the cup he said, "Pretty little thing, wasn't she?"

"Yes, she was. But quick-tempered."

"Why did she rob the bank?"

Whit explained about the dead outlaw she'd intended to marry down in Arizona. Doctor Muller gently wagged his head. "She was too pretty to get hitched to someone like that."

Whit reached for his cup, tasted it, went to the cupboard, and returned with his whiskey bottle. They both tipped a little popskull into the cups. Whit said, "Carl, you'd ought to hire on with the Pinkertons."

Muller chuckled. "I told you, in my business a man learns to notice things. I been at my trade about as many years as you are old. It's just sort of second nature with me . . . This is good coffee. Did she scrub the kitchen and the coffeepot too?"

"Yeah. While she waited for nightfall." Whit leaned on the table. "Jack will have a fit."

Muller's cup was poised halfway when it stopped moving. "Given? Why should he have a fit? There's something else I can tell you about doctors, Whit. I don't believe there was ever a doctor born who didn't go into his grave with more confidences than you could shake a stick at. By the time Marshal Given is back on the job, this other thing will be just about forgotten. Something will have come along to recatch public interest. As far as I'm concerned only two people really suffered—Charley Bonner and Jake Spooner. Charley's his old self again. Jake, well, he'll rob the next person he trades horses with. Right now I've got to get back up to the house or Jack'll be trying to get out of bed to feed himself. Did you know I was a pretty fair cook?"

Whit did not know that. As they both arose he said, "I'll remember that the next time I get hurt . . . Carl?"

"Forget it. I already have. I hope she made it to—wherever she went. I hope she learned a lesson." Muller thrust out a big hand. "This ends it, right here in your kitchen. You and I know. No one else ever will, and you and I would do well to forget it."

After the doctor's departure Whit returned to the table to finish his laced coffee. During their talk he had progressed through just about every emotion he could name, beginning with apprehension, to guilt, to acute discomfort, to fear, to gradual astonishment, and finally to relief.

He finished the coffee, got another cupful, laced it, and sat at the table until the afternoon was waning, then he cleaned up the kitchen, went out back to scrub, and strolled up to the café for an early supper, because if he was going to take out the dawn southbound for Sam Holt, he would need a decent night's sleep.

25

Later, Much Later

IN time it got to the point where Sam could not read manifests without using a big magnifying glass, so he took to carrying the glass around with him. Doctor Muller told Whit it was simply a matter of time before Sam would be unable to distinguish anything except light and dark.

But Sam was a stubborn—or desperate—individual. He hung on until there just was no way for him to continue. He sold the stage company to Whit Pierson, who secured a loan for the purchase from Charley Bonner.

Jake Spooner had a heart attack one bitterly cold winter day shortly after Christmas. He lingered for two days, then died.

Buffler Stoneman bought the livery barn; had been riding shotgun for the stage company since Jack Given had returned to his lawman's job. Jack did fairly well, but he told Whit the following year that he was just then beginning to feel completely recovered.

Walt Coggins took in a partner at the general store. Walt had gotten heavy; his feet bothered him if he was on them all day. Besides, he no longer had to work ten hours a day. He and his wife took one of Whit's stages down to Livermore, where they took one of the steam cars to some hot-water place over in Texas where it was said problems like the ones bothering Charley could be cured.

Doughbelly, Tom Hart, and Whit Pierson established the habit of playing poker every Friday night, and continued to do so for three years. They probably would have done it for another three years but Doughbelly and old Mike Flaherty entered into a partnership that required Doughbelly to ride one of Whit's stages down to Livermore every week to keep an eye on their slaughterhouse down there, and each time Doughbelly returned he slept like a log for a full night and day. He hadn't been a young man for quite a spell.

Carl Muller took Doughbelly's place at the Friday-night poker sessions. He gave up cigars four years after the bank robbery, saying that something was beginning to bother his throat and while he did not want to think his stogies were responsible, he thought he'd give them up for a while anyway. What he neglected to say was that he'd read an article in a medical journal stating that cigars had caused the death of President Grant some years back, and because the symptoms were the same, what he had read had scared the hell out of him.

Whit never married. His Beaverton Stage & Cartage Company prospered. He was able to pay off his loan at Bonner's bank within four years.

He paid his whips well and hired on gun-guards whenever he thought it advisable to do so. He discontinued Sam Holt's practice of buying only combination horses. When asked about this occasionally, usually by his yardmen and drivers, he would simply say he had personal reasons for wanting only horses that could *not* be ridden as well as driven.

One brilliant day in early summer about five years after Jake Spooner's funeral, Doctor Muller ambled into the corralyard office. He had just come from Coggins's store after picking up his mail. He had been asked by a clerk to take Whit's mail to him, since Muller would have to pass the corralyard office on his way home.

Whit was standing by the roadway window, soaking up the sun's warmth, when Muller entered. Whit had seen him coming and greeted the doctor with a smile. "Nice day," he said.

Muller nodded in agreement and handed Whit his mail. He watched Whit examine the envelope.

Muller took a chair beside the window, got comfortable, and told Whit, "Open it."

Whit sat down at his desk, put everything aside but the small, tan envelope, and slit it with a wicked-bladed boot knife lying atop the desk.

Muller folded both hands in his lap, waiting. "Did I ever tell you that Charley showed me and Buffler Stoneman that brown paper the bank money was wrapped in six years ago?"

Whit leaned on the desk, holding a folded letter, as he answered. "No, you never did."

Muller jutted his jaw. "Same handwriting, Whit."

For a moment the only noise in the office was made by a laden dray wagon grinding out on the corralyard into the roadway. "Well, are you going to read it or just sit there like you saw a ghost?" Muller asked.

Whit looked down, read the letter, which was not very long, then glanced across the room at Carl Muller. "You want to know?" he asked softly.

"Of course. Why do you think I'm sitting here?"

Whit looked down again. " 'Dear Whit. I did not stop in Arizona. I rode all the way to California. Three years ago I married a wonderful man who owns a shipping business. We have two children. One I named for my mother—Cynthia. The little boy I named Whitney. I have never forgotten and I never will. If you ever visit San Francisco I want very much for you to come and see me.' "

Muller waited a moment, then asked if she had signed it. Whit nodded. "Yeah. 'Mrs. Henry Willingham.' The address is a place called Nob Hill." He put the letter down very gently as Doctor Muller got heavily out of the chair and turned toward the door.

"Whit, I been delivering babies forty years and so help me not once has anyone named one after me. You—well—I think that was really appropriate of her. If you ever go out to San Francisco . . ."

Whit stood up at his desk. "If I ever go out to San Francisco, Carl, I'll be a hell of a lot older than I am now, and even then, I won't do it. Remember what you said in my kitchen years ago? It's finished."

Muller smiled from the doorway. "She liked you."

"And I liked her, and leaves fall every autumn an' the wind blows 'em every which way, an' that's how people are. Carl?"

"Yes."

"Is today Friday?"

"Tomorrow is Friday."

"See you at the poker table tomorrow evening."

Muller was still smiling when he nodded and walked back out into the sunshine.

Lauran Paine who, under his own name and various pseudonyms has written over 900 books, was born in Duluth, Minnesota. His family moved to California when he was at an early age and his apprenticeship as a Western writer came about through the years he spent in the livestock trade, rodeos, and even motion pictures—where he served as an extra because of his expert horsemanship in several films starring movie cowboy Johnny Mack Brown. In the late 1930s, Paine trapped wild horses in northern Arizona and, for a time, worked as a professional farrier. Paine came to know the old West through the eyes of many who had been born in the previous century and he learned that Western life had been very different from the way it was portrayed on the screen. "I knew men who had killed other men," he later recalled. "But they were the exceptions. Prior to and during the Depression, people were just too busy eking out an existence to indulge in Saturday-night brawls." He served in the U.S. Navy in the Second World War and began writing for Western pulp magazines following his discharge. It is interesting to note that all of his earliest novels (written under his own name and the pseudonym Mark Carrel) were published in the British market and he soon had as strong a following in that country as in the United States. Paine's Western fiction is characterized by strong plots, authenticity, an apparently effortless ability to construct situation and character, and a preference for building his stories upon a solid foundation of historical fact. *Adobe Empire* (1956), one of his best novels, is a fictionalized account of the last twenty years in the life of trader William Bent and, in an off-trail way, has a melancholy, bittersweet texture that is not easily forgotten. In later novels like *The White Bird* (1997) and *Cache Cañon* (1998), he showed that the special magic and power of his stories and characters had only matured along with his basic themes of changing times, changing attitudes, learning from experience, respecting Nature, and the yearning for a simpler, more moderate way of life. The film *Open Range* (Buena Vista, 2003), based on Paine's 1990 novel, starring Robert Duvall, Kevin Costner, and Annette Bening became an international success.